REBEL RAIDERS

A gang of former Confederate soldiers is robbing and killing its way across Kansas. Novice lawman Cass Clacy is sent out after them, but what chance does he have of outgunning such experienced fighters? When Sheriff Jim Clarke joins Cass in the chase, his main aim is a share of the reward. Together they penetrate deep into the heart of the Indian Nations, where Cass falls under the spell of the lovely Audrey — but can he save her from the clutches of the dangerous Josiah Baines?

JOHN DYSON

REBEL RAIDERS

Complete and Unabridged

LINFORD
Leicester

First published in Great Britain in 2013 by
Robert Hale Limited
London

First Linford Edition
published 2015
by arrangement with
Robert Hale Limited
London

A catalogue record for this book is available
from the British Library.

ISBN 978–1–4448–2354–7

Published by
F. A. Thorpe (Publishing)
Anstey, Leicestershire

Set by Words & Graphics Ltd.
Anstey, Leicestershire
Printed and bound in Great Britain by
T. J. International Ltd., Padstow, Cornwall

This book is printed on acid-free paper

To Audrey
The sweetest girl in the world
In loving memory

J.D.

1

The first thing Cass Clacy knew was a hammering at the door as he surfaced from the depths of sleep and Mary Molineux beside him, half-naked in her skimpy slip, hissing, as she leaned over him, 'Cass, it's my husband.'

'Your husband?' he grunted. 'What's he want? What you doin' here?'

'Don't you remember?' Mary's face amid her unkempt hair was distraught. 'You . . . me . . . last night . . . we came back.'

'Did we?' The hammering at the door was intensifying. Luckily it was solid oak and bolted, but vibrating alarmingly as if the man outside was trying to shoulder it in. Cass spotted an empty whiskey bottle on the floor. 'Oh, yuh. So we did.'

'What are we going to do?' Mary whispered, fearfully hanging on to him, her soft, warm, milk-white body press-ing close.

The young Texan detached himself from her limpet embrace, rolled out of bed, pulled on his blue jeans, stood bare-foot and bare-chested, and reached for the revolver in his gunbelt hanging from a chair.

'No, please! Don't kill him,' Mary moaned. 'Think of my kids.'

Suddenly an iron crowbar cracked through a panel of the door with such splintering force she, too, leaped off the mattress. 'Where can I hide?'

Cass shushed her with a forefinger, pointed to a half-open window. 'On the roof,' he hissed in her ear. 'I'll try an' get rid of him.'

'Oh, God!' To make ends meet Mary worked in the evenings as cashier behind the bar at Eureka city's main saloon. 'Why didn't I go home?'

The crowbar smashed through the door again, making them both almost jump out of their skins. She gave him a wild, doubtful look of panic as the crowbar waggled back and forth. She snatched up her bits and pieces, skirt, shoes, blouse, hat and handbag, bundled them into her shawl, clambered on to the chair and tried to climb through the small window. But her wide buttocks got stuck fast. Cass gave her bouncy butts a shove and she tumbled out on to the veranda, as Bill Molineux roared, 'Open up!'

The attic room was three storeys up at the top of a solid Victorian edifice that had once been a hotel when the town had known better days but was now a run-down warren of rooms to let.

Mary clambered precariously on to the balcony wall and tried to haul herself up on to the steep, shingled roof, her bare toes kicking desperately to find purchase. Cass braced himself and went to the door which was suddenly split apart and he came face to face through the crack with the irate eyes of her husband.

'Hiya, Bill,' Cass drawled. 'What'n hell ya doin' to my door?' He slid back the bolt and opened up. 'You gawn mad or sumpun?'

The burly Molineux pushed him aside, bursting into the room, looking around perplexed, like a maddened bull. 'Where is she? Mary? I know she's here.'

'What?' Cass stepped back out of reach of the iron bar Molineux brandished, but lowered his revolver. 'How do I know where she is? What's wrong?'

Bill had an unhealthy pallor, his face glistening with sweat beneath his greasy black hair. He strode from side to side, peering under the bed, jerking open the wardrobe door as if he might find her inside. But all that clattered out were empty bottles.

'I been meaning to git rid of them,' Cass muttered.

'She's been out all night. She ain't been home. They said at the saloon she left with you. What you done with her?'

'Me? I ain't done nuthin'. We parted outside. I thought she was going home.'

'Oh, yeah?' Bill stood over him, the bar raised, as if tempted to strike out.

'Don't do nuthin' stupid, Bill. She's probably at her sister's.'

'No, I've been out there. They ain't seen her.'

'Well, she ain't here neither.'

'If I catch that woman I'll give her what for,' Bill thundered, as he stuck his head out the window and gaped around. 'She'll taste the leather of my belt.'

'See! She ain't out on the balcony.' Cass suddenly spotted one of Mary's black stockings snaking out of the blankets. He quickly pocketed it, and glanced about for any other giveaways. 'Take a look on the roof, if ya want.'

Molineux didn't accept the invitation but turned, shaking his head as if dismayed and his voice cracked. 'Where's she gotten to?'

'Come on, pal. You need a drink.' Cass hurriedly pulled on his shirt, boots and gunbelt, grabbing his hat and headed through the shattered door. 'I'll forget about the damage. You're a tad upset. Any man would be.'

Bill followed him, clattering down the narrow, uncarpeted stairways until they reached Eureka's dirt street and then he walked beside his fellow deputy marshal along towards the saloon.

'I expect she'll be home when you git back,' Cassius consoled, turning and looking back to see the frail figure of Mary perched on the roof clutching her clothes to her with one arm as she hung on to the chimney stack with the other, the cold prairie wind whipping through her flaxen hair.

He gave her a finger-fluttering backhand wave.

'Jeez, is that the time?' he said, as he pushed through the batwing doors of the Red Garter and saw the hands of the clock standing at ten to ten. 'I musta had a skinful.' There were a couple of the customary early morning drinkers and a distinguished-looking gent with white hair, moustachios and goatee beard, a caped riding coat, and glass in hand, standing at the bar. Looked like he'd just blown in, cattle-dealer or some sort.

The barkeep didn't need to ask. He set up a bottle and two half-pint tumblers for them. Cass poured two strong shots and they drank in silence.

'Don't be too hard on her, Bill. A woman ain't like a hoss you can whip into submission. Well, Mary ain't. I was talking to her in here last night as she was finishing her shift and it sounded like you and her are having a few problems. You start in larruping her and she may go for good. Mary's a spunky gal.'

Maybe that was the wrong wordage for Molineux grabbed him by the shirt front, spilling his drink, his ugly mug half-an-inch from Cass's face. 'You keep out of my affairs, Clacy. If I ever hear of you speaking to my wife again I'll — '

Just what he would do, however, was voided by the blast of an explosion from the bank across the road and the sound of gunfire. 'Christ!' he shouted, dropping Cass, 'What the hell's happening?'

'Sounds like we're under attack,' Cass replied. 'Damn, and I ain't got my carbine. Anybody got a rifle?'

'Yeah, I have!' Joe, the 'keep, pulled a Sharps single shot from under the bar, and ran over to the window. 'And it looks like I need it.'

'Hot damn!' Bill Molineux was exasperated. 'I ain't armed. Anybody else got a gun?' But there was no reply from the other men in the saloon. The white-haired stranger just kept sipping his whiskey.

'They're robbing the bank,' Joe hollered, 'There's one feller there holding the horses.'

Cass parted the net curtain with the barrel of his Marlin 'Never Miss' .38. 'We need to take him out then they'll have nuthin' for the getaway. Can you get a bead on him?'

'Sure.' Joe poked the carbine barrel out and squinted along the sights. 'If the danged horses would stay still a second.'

The solid, brick-built bank building was about forty yards away diagonally across the street. Black smoke from the explosion was trickling out of its door and the noise had obviously startled the mustangs. They were plunging and whinnying, trying to drag away.

'Come on, give it your best shot,' Cass urged, for he couldn't be sure of an accurate aim with his handgun. 'I'm going out on to the sidewalk to get in closer.'

As he spoke half-a-dozen men ran from the front entrance of the bank, gunny-sacks and guns in their hands, looking around them, fanning out.

'It's the Rebel Raiders,' Bill shouted, for all the men were attired in versions of the uniform of the former Confederate Army. 'They ain't s'posed to be in these parts.'

'Well they're sure here, ain't they?' Cass cried, as the 'keep wildly released his shot which, instead of hitting the horse-holder, bowled over an old lady in a big hat who was standing behind the gang. 'Shee-it! Look what you done now.'

Alarmed, the bank robbers took cover behind wagons, a horse trough and posts and sent a blazing volley of lead smashing through the glass and frame of the window. Cass ducked desperately for cover as bullets screamed past his head, ricocheting about the saloon.

Screwing up his eyes he returned to the attack firing his 'Never Miss' out of the window, but amid all the smoke and bedlam he couldn't see if he had missed or not. Then his five shots were gone. 'I need to get out there closer,' he gritted out, kneeling back to reload from his belt.

'There's one of 'em on his horse,' Joe shouted, waving his rifle about. 'I cain't miss this time.'

'Well, hit him,' Cass replied. 'For God's sake — '

But, as he glanced back at the bar the distinguished gent, Colonel Cody lookalike, was dragging out a long-barrelled Remington from under his riding coat and aimed it point blank at Joe's back. The barkeep gave a howl and collapsed.

The Marlin's drop-down cylinder was dropped down, so Cass had no choice and a split second to roll away as 'Cody', yelling some words, side-stepped away towards the saloon door, the Remington blazing lead. Bill hurled a chair at him, but the man fended it away with his free arm before putting a bullet in his attacker's leg and dodging away through the batwings.

By the time Cass had righted himself, reloaded the five-shot and dashed out to the sidewalk, the gang had gained their saddles, whirling their mounts and firing at anyone who showed them-selves. The town butcher had come out of his shop with a shotgun but was blasted back into his doorway. Then, led by their debonair 'colonel', the robbers galloped away down the street.

All Cass could do was to send a few

unavailing .38s after them and watch them wheel around a corner and disappear. His first thought was to find his horse and go after them, but what chance would one man have, even if he caught up with them, against seven desperate shootists?

Instead, he ran back to the old lady spreadeagled on the sidewalk, her boots pointing heavenwards. 'Why didn't you get outa the way?' he admonished, but she was unable to reply. Her bonnet had rolled away and her white hair was neatly netted. A genteel look of lavender and lace about her. He had seen her pottering about, talking to herself as many of the old and lonesome do. Her blue eyes wide, she stared at him, helplessly. 'Somebody get the doc,' he called, but he knew it was too late. 'We'll catch up with him,' he vowed, 'the man responsible for this. One day, I promise you.' She tried to nod her wrinkled, kindly face, but choked on her own blood which suddenly poured in a black ooze from her mouth. She fell back and Cass sadly shook his head, closed her eyes, and wondered why he had made that empty lawman's boast. Was it to comfort her?

But his head was spinning from the sudden events and his hangover. Three down, all apparently dead, with Molineux wailing about his leg. What he needed was another stiff drink.

★ ★ ★

'What the hell were you doing strolling around town without a gun?' Marshal Brad Brady bellowed at Bill Molineux, who was still down on the saloon floor-boards, Doc Rossiter applying a tourniquet to his thigh, trying to stop the blood flow. 'You're s'posed to be a lawman not a damn civilian.'

'I was off-duty,' Molineux whined. 'It was *his* fault.'

'Who?' the overweight and sweaty Brady demanded. 'What you talking about?'

'*Him*.' Bill nodded at Cass. 'That

bastard. If I'd had a gun I'd have killed him. So I didn't take one.'

'What's Clacy got to do with it?'

'Aw, he's got some crazy idea I was sniffin' after his missus.' Cass shrugged. 'I ain't that sorta guy.'

'It's *his* fault.' Bill groaned, as the bandage was jerked tight. 'If I'd had got a gun I could have dropped a couple of those killers.'

'Missus? Sniffin'? What *are* you two, dimwits? Schoolkids? You're supposed to be responsible law enforcers. There's three innocent townspeople shot dead in front of you and all you can do is whinge about your sex life, or lack of it, whichever's the case. No wonder my department gets no respect. I might remind you there's an election coming up. You two could well be out of a job.'

'Yeah,' Molineux murmured, surlily. 'So could you.'

'This is all very well,' Cass intervened. 'Ain't it time we got a posse organized and went after them?'

'What, and see more innocent civilians slaughtered?' Brady roared. 'Why didn't either of you two nincompoops challenge the older guy? He was an obvious stranger in town.'

'I dunno. Maybe you're right. He looked kinda respectable to me. A dead ringer for that famous Colonel Cody guy. The one who runs the circus.'

'Oh, my God,' Brady groaned. 'Circus? Cody? That man was indeed a colonel. You got that bit right. The *in*famous Colonel John G. Anderson. Ain't you seen his mugshot on the Wanted posters?'

'Oh!' Cass tipped his Stetson over his nose and scratched the back of his head. '*That* colonel. I knew he looked familiar.'

'What a coupla fools!' Brady exploded. 'Huccome I got you two ninnies on my hands? What did I do to deserve this? What's the mayor gonna say?'

Cass had to agree that to try to raise a posse from a few eager but inexperienced storekeepers might not be a good idea. He had tried before with dire results. And he doubted if any local ranchers would be keen to lend their cowhands for support. It was their busy time of year: the spring round-up.

He remembered the colonel's words spat out as he headed for the door. '*What have them Yankee bankers ever done for you boys?*' A lot of southern folk felt that way.

'He had a point,' he muttered, more to himself.

'What?' the stentorian Brady demanded.

'Aw, nuthin'. But just what *are* we going to do?'

'You're going after 'em,' Brady said. 'Alone.'

2

The Rebel Raiders, as they were known for a previous attack in the north of the state, charged on their way at a pounding lope, the blood-red flag of the Confederacy, with its St Andrew's cross of thirteen stars, flying at their head, held by Jed, a boy with a face red raw with acne. They planned to cut a swathe across this south-east corner of Kansas before night came. They had three other calls in mind. For thirty-five miles they rode before easing their horses in to give them a break outside the next town of Eldorado.

'No sign of pursuit.' Another of the three younger men in their group, Mace Underwood, yelled joyously. He was wearing his long-dead father's grey frock coat, a lieutenant's rank on the epaulettes and the parental campaign hat, a red cockade pinned to one side.

'These backwoods 'peckers know better'n to give us any trouble,' Skeeter Hardy, their oldest member, replied. His face beneath his forage cap was as wrinkled as a rooster's claw, every crease ingrained with dirt.

'Right, y'all listen to me,' Colonel John G. Anderson snapped. 'Too much blood was shed back there. It was indeed her own fault, but that old lady getting smithereened is not good publicity for our righteous cause. We want folks to regard us as friends, liberators from the northern yoke, not enemies.'

'She shouldn't have got in the way. Nor that stupid butcher. He was gonna let us have it with both barrels 'fore I changed his tune.' The speaker was a tall, sinewy man, his face gaunt beneath the peaked cap of a former Louisiana regiment. He had ridden with Anderson since the troubles of '59 and all through the war. 'Here y'are, J.G., this should cheer you up. I done made a count of three thousand, eight hundred

18

and ninety-two dollars.' He tossed him a gunny-sack. 'You wanna check it?'

'I trust you implicitly, Josiah,' Anderson proclaimed, as he caught the bag. 'These funds will aid our noble cause.'

'Yup,' Josiah Baines loosened his mount's girth and let the horse lap at the stream a bit. He gave a mocking smile. 'They sho' will.'

'The butcher's death was justifiable self-defence.' Anderson's long white hair blew in the wind and he stroked it to one side of his sour countenance as he continued to lecture them. 'I regret I, too, had to put a bullet into a bartender in the saloon. He was about to put one in the back of young Jed here.'

'Aw. These dang mustangs takes some hangin' on to,' the spotty-faced youth whined. 'I done my best, suh.'

'Keep your eyes skinned, that's all I'm saying. My own are getting a bit hazy these days and I must admit I nearly put a slug in someone I glimpsed up on a roof. Thought it was a sniper, but it was some half-naked woman hanging to a chimney breast.'

'What'n hail was she doin' up there?' Skeeter asked, as the men guffawed.

'Gentlemen, you will ride into Eldorado in an hour's time at exactly noon. You have my permission to fall out. Check your armaments and ammunition, see to your mounts and relax for an hour. I, of course, will be there twenty minutes before you. If you hear my warning shot, or other shots, abort the mission. Don't worry about me. That's an order. I'm well prepared to die for the cause.'

Anderson turned to a plumper character, Randy Sims, their safe-cracker. 'How many sticks of dynamite we got left?'

'Enough,' Sims smirked. 'But if I go up in smoke in the saddle you'll know why. It ain't exactly the most stable substance to be galloping around with.'

★　★　★

Before he could go after the robbers Cass had to disperse the rubber-neckers outside the bank, scoop up the old lady who had got in the line of fire, drag out poor Joe by his bootheels, and go check the butcher, An unerring heart-shot from one of the robbers had sent him back-pedalling to land in a tub of pig's guts where he reclined, his eyes like dead clams. 'Yuk!' Cass hauled him out and carted the three corpses over to the funeral parlour.

Eureka, as its name implied, had once been the site of a gold strike and for a few glory days a boom town. Nowadays, however, it was a generally peaceful south Kansas town with, apart from a couple of brick buildings, mostly wooden frame houses and stores.

The town had, as they said, got a bad case of the respectables, goodtime girls who once flocked there banned by by-law from soliciting in the streets and saloons. The flagrant fragrance of the few who remained could now only be sniffed in a ramshackle honky-tonk on the outskirts of town.

Marshal Brady, of course, had not lent Cass a hand. He preferred to keep his fat backside planted in his comfortable office chair and attend to paperwork. Cass found him ensconced in a coffee shop with the town mayor. Both were getting stuck into a breakfast of ham and eggs. 'This attack came completely outa the blue,' Brady spluttered, as egg yolk trickled down his fat chins. 'It caught my boys on the hop. But, don't fret, I'm sending Cass here, my best man, to retrieve that stolen four thousand dollars.'

The mayor gave Cass a withering look and growled, 'Sure, and pigs might fly.'

'Well, what you waiting for?' Brady snapped. 'Go interview them in the bank. Get any descriptions you can. Then git after them boys tomorrow, first light of dawn. You gotta infiltrate.'

'Infiltrate?'

'Yes, go under cover. Join the gang. You're a Texan southerner, aincha?

Find out what they're up to, then tip me off so we can be ready and waiting for their next strike.'

'You sure make it sound easy,' Cass drawled. 'I ain't even had time for a wash and shave yet, let alone git my socks on.'

'That reminds me. You'd better get yourself tidied up 'cause in spite of what's happened Judge Ross will still be holding court. You got that drunk and Molly McGinty to git outa the cells and put up before him. So snap to it, Clacy.'

'Sure,' Cass sighed. 'Anything else?'

'No. I'll cover the inquests on them three poor souls.' Brady went back to stuffing his face. 'You are allowed five cents a mile travelling expenses. Don't forget to keep me informed.'

Cass decided to put off his ablutions to later, headed for the jail and ushered his prisoners into the adjoining courthouse. The officious Bill Molineux had made the arrest the day before when Molly and her customer were blatantly carousing in the town.

Since then the brassy 'assisted-blonde', Molly McGinty had been kicking up such a din in the cells they needed to be rid of her. Judge Ross frowned at the ill-attired Cass and heard the evidence. 'You're fined twenty dollars,' he told Molly. 'Pay up, or it's a month inside.'

'Gimme bail, Judge, an' I'll have ya fine hustled up in a coupla nights. Maybe you'd like to indulge yourself? Very reasonable rates, satisfaction guaranteed.'

The judge harrumphed, asking his clerk, 'What's she on about?'

After a whispered conversation Ross announced, 'Case adjourned two weeks. Bail granted in the prisoner's own recognisance of ten dollars. Take her away.'

'Thank you, Judge,' Molly yelled, swinging her scarlet parasol. 'See ya around.'

Luckily there wasn't much else and the court closed. Now he had to go hire a buggy and pair and haul Bill Molineux out of the saloon and settle him in the driving seat. He could find his own way home. He would be laid up for a while with his wounded leg. 'At least he won't be able to knock Mary around,' Cass reflected, assuming she had picked up her three children from her sister's and gone back to the family abode by now.

'You get all the luck, doncha?' Molineux groaned, as he stuck out his injured leg and grabbed the reins Cass handed him. 'How much bounty is there on those guys? Why should you get all the malooka?'

'There ain't any guarantee I'm gonna get anything 'cept a bullet in the gut. Hagh!' Cass whacked his hat at the pair and set them speeding off, Bill hanging on for dear life. 'Maybe now I can git some grub and a tub and relax.'

He soaked in a barrel of hot suds back of the barber's shop, but in the restaurant folks kept buttonholing him wanting to know what role he'd played in the shootings. So he went to see to his horse and packed a few essentials, bullets and beef-jerky and suchlike, for the trip.

* ★ ★ ★

It had been Colonel John Anderson's baptism of fire. He had been a young man then back in '59. He stood beneath the maple trees, their fresh leaves caressed by the breeze and recalled those brutal days, the cruelties inflicted by both sides. They called his bunch the Border Ruffians, and he guessed they were ruffians, men like Josiah Baines who would slice his blade across an animal or human throat without a second of remorse. They had to be brutal. They were pro-slavery. They had their way of life to defend. Anderson owned a plantation in Louisiana with fifty slaves. They weren't free but he prided himself they were well looked after. Anderson had come to the Kansas-Missouri border to fight the thieves who would steal their slaves, their livelihood; the so-called Free State men, the abolitionists. Anderson called them Jayhawkers for like all jayhawks they would steal from other nests. Thieves and ignoramuses, in his opinion. It had been bitter fighting. And the bitterness still remained, especially in Anderson's heart.

Nowadays, this place, Eldorado, with its maple trees lining the street, was just another optimistically named hick town. And at high noon it had a tranquil air. There were a few scrubby cowponies tethered outside the Last Chance saloon. Farming families loaded supplies on their wagons at the grainstore.

Anderson smoked a cheroot, thickset in his caped riding coat and wide-brimmed hat. If anybody had looked closely they would have seen the bulk of his sidearm beneath the coat. There was no danger. Just a bunch of rowdy cowboys in the saloon. The colonel had had a beer and passed the time of day. 'What brings you to our little town, suh?' the barkeep had asked.

'I'm here on business,' Anderson replied.

Twelve noon, precisely. Anderson consulted his gold fobwatch. He was a stickler for punctuality. Where had they got to? He prided himself that he planned every operation with military precision. Ah, here they were, clipping across the log bridge which was trussed by rope over a stream and heading into town. One or two of the shoppers stared at them, but assumed they were just drovers off the trail, their clothes swathed with white dust. Anderson himself gave no sign of recognition as they cantered by. He watched them jump down outside Regan's Bank, toss their reins to Spotty Jed, as they called him, pull bandannas high to cover their faces, and push inside. He strolled along to stand behind his own hitched horse, nodding 'howdy' to two men who passed.

There was a queue of three people inside the bank at the teller's window, the first a blowsy woman in a big,

28

flower-decorated hat. The owner of a ladies millinery, she was paying in some cash she held in her hand.

'I'll have that, sweetheart.' Josiah Baines closed his strong fist over hers, claimed the money, and stuck the barrel of his blued-steel Colt into her ample bosom.

Simultaneously, two of his colleagues, Jawbone Hudson and Whispering Rick, as they were known, moved in on the two other customers, frisking them, snatching their valuables and wallets, and waving them into a corner. 'Get down on your damn knees,' Jawbone bellowed. 'Any of you Jayhawkers wanna stay alive you won't make a peep.'

Young Mace Underwood pushed in front of the woman, stuck his revolver through the grille, and smiled at the clerk. 'You wanna see another sunrise, mister, you better hand over the keys to the safe.'

The clerk stared at him like a petrified mouse beneath the gaze of a hovering hawk. 'I don't have them, sir,' he stuttered. 'Mr Regan has them. He's along at the saloon.'

'You're lying. Unbolt the gate.' Mace indicated the teller to open the wire-mesh access to the back office and shoved through. There were wads of notes and gold coin in the teller's drawer which Mace stuffed into the capacious pockets of his grey frock coat. But there were no keys to be found.

'This is outrageous,' the woman squawked, as Josiah, in his forage cap with the crossed swords, squeezed her back against the corner wall and groped grimy fingers into her costume, ripping open the buttons of her blouse. 'Nice ones,' he cackled, as he found her warm naked breasts and nipples.

'You better get to work, Randy,' Skeeter shouted.

'No problem,' the tubby little Sims replied, surveying the big iron safe in the backroom. 'I'll have this open in a trice.' He twiddled the combination dial to no effect. 'Ah, well,' he drawled, 'we're gonna have to blow this thang. You better take cover, boys.'

Mace and the others retreated and squatted with the teller and customers behind the counter. Randy struck matches, lit the short fuses. 'Come on, my li'l babies,' he crooned.

He scrambled on to the top of the safe, swinging up his short legs. Beneath it the fuses hissed ominously.

Outside Anderson fumed. 'Why are they taking so long?' But suddenly there was a muffled explosion from inside the bank.

Josiah had the struggling woman on the floor, trying to get his groping hand up under her long skirts. 'Thar she blows!' He grinned as the walls shook to the blast. He shoved the revolver into the woman's mouth and licked his tongue lasciviously up her cheek. She grimaced, appalled.

'Beautiful!' Randy cried, hopping down and peering through the drifting smoke at the safe door hanging wide.

But the proceeds were far from

beautiful to Mace as he scraped cash from the shelves. 'Four hundred lousy stinkin' dollars,' he screamed. 'Where's the rest?'

'Mr Regan ain't been doing so well,' the clerk cried. 'To tell the truth he's got a big gambling habit.'

'What, uses the customers' cash?' Mace said. 'The double-crossing toerag. That ain't nice.' He shovelled what there was into a sack. 'Aw, come on. We're wasting our time.'

'You're coming with me, honey.' With a grip of steel, the lean-hipped Josiah hauled the lady, her hat askew, up in front of him and out of the bank, using her as a shield.

A bunch of cowhands were tumbling from the Eldorado saloon, going for their guns, but Josiah pushed the milliner towards them, letting loose with his .45, covering the boys as they scrambled on to their plunging mustangs. Fearlessly, he faced the cowhands' fire, sent two of them spinning back into the dust as his partners thundered past him, shooting wildly at any who were in the way, scattering them like ducks.

Josiah gave the woman a wet kiss on the lips. 'So long, sweetheart.' He hurled her at the cowhands and she teetered forward and screamed as a bullet hit her hard.

'Here y'are,' Spotty Jed hollered, galloping up the street with a mustang in tow.

Josiah grabbed the saddle horn and swung aboard like some circus acrobat, as Anderson brought up the rear, his sidearm in his hand and cocked for action. But the opposition had lost heart, dodging for cover, and he followed his men out across the bridge, and heading away down the trail. 'On to Wichita!' he cried.

★   ★   ★

Back in Eureka, Cass sat in the jail office scratching with a quill pen. 'Before you go,' Brady had told him, 'notify the next of kin of them three fatalities.' Easier said than done. Rumour was the old widow lady had relatives back in New England. Cass was fretting at the leash, wanting to get after the robbers but it looked like he'd be delayed. He hurled the pen aside in frustration and about ten o'clock decided to have an early night.

'What the hell are you doing here?'

Through his open door he saw a stockinged, white-thighed leg swinging tantalizingly from the edge of the bed.

Mary smiled up at him brightly. 'That's a fine welcome. Bill's disabled so he can't stop me coming to see you, can he? I told him I'd got to work at the Garter, but it's my night off.'

Cass stood and scowled at her. 'Look, this ain't no good. You're a married woman. You got your kids to think of. You gotta forget me.'

'Darling Cass, don't be such a prude.' Mary put up her arms, pleadingly. 'Give me a kiss. I won't stay long. Just an hour or so.'

His intended quick kiss turned into a long one as she murmured 'Mmm!' and pulled him down on top of her. And the hour became two hours as they lay in each other's arms.

'I'm going to leave him. I can't stand his blows. You don't know what it's like. He knocked me downstairs t'other day. I got my own back. I slammed the door on his fingers. I'll run away with you, Cass.'

'What about your kids?'

'Oh, he'll soon find some other skivvy to look after him and them. Cass,' she pleaded, 'we can't miss this chance. It's the first time I've ever felt so good in bed with a man.'

'Must be my magic fingers,' he mused, as he gently stroked her. 'No, it ain't no good. I can't do that to Bill.'

But the bedsprings began to creak rhthymically and soon her husband was forgotten. 'Well, you don't seem to mind doing this to me.' She laughed wantonly.

'This is different. Coupla hours now

and again,' he panted. 'Why don't we leave it like this?' He slumped down on her, exhausted. 'Whoo!'

They lay there silent for a while, breathing hard, until he disentangled himself. 'Anyway,' he said. 'I got to go after those robbers. Don't know when or if I'll be back.'

'Why? Why do you have to spoil it? Why do you have to risk your life for a few lousy dollars?'

'It's better'n cow-punching.'

'What, being a lousy lawman? And, another thing, why did you tell Bill to take a look on the roof? That was pushing things, wasn't it? What if he had?'

'But he didn't, did he? That was a bluff. Like in poker.'

'Bluff.' She sat up back against the pillow and lit a cigarette. 'You certainly got some funny ideas.'

'Aw, come on, Mary. If I catch those guys there might be a big reward. If there is I'll split it with Bill. He ain't so bad.'

'He's a pig. Why don't we just go, light out for Colorado or someplace. Now's our chance. We'll have a three weeks' head start on him. He'll never find us.'

'Nah.' He rolled over her and out of bed. 'I can't do that.'

'Why not, Cass?' she begged. 'This is our one chance of happiness.'

'No. We better get dressed, Mary. I'll see you home.'

3

For five years Abilene, in the north-east of the state, had been the biggest boom town in Kansas, shipping out on its railroad one and half million Texas long-horns to the meat markets of the Eastern cities. But with the opening of the Atchison, Topeka and Santa Fe line which cut across the south of the state Newton and Wichita had taken over the mantle as the cowboys brought their herds up the Chisholm Trail.

Sheriff Jim Clarke had done well for himself, as the randy, thirsty and gambling-crazy Texans flocked into Wichita's new and numerous saloons at beef-packing time. The upright citizens of his town council, to encourage him in his activities, had decreed that he could take a cut or a 'bonus' of all fines imposed for the flouting of by-laws ranging from forbidding fast riding in town, brawling and blaspheming, to immoral behaviour and prostitution.

But now, in the year of 1874, it looked like Wichita's star was on the wane, too, for a new branch line had opened going another forty miles south to Caldwell, almost on the borders of Indian Territory. Why would the Texan ranchers want to drive their herds further north if they didn't need to? 'We've had a good run, boys,' Clarke told his deputies. 'But it looks like it might be over.'

However, Wichita's stores were still doing a busy trade even out of season, and, as Colonel John Anderson and his men cantered their horses in, crossing the railroad line, passing the half-empty corrals and clipping along main street, they were greeted by hordes of gaily-dressed prairie nymphs hanging over the balconies of parlour rooms above saloons, smiling painted lips with shrill and saucy invitations to join them.

Josiah grinned and waved up to

them, like a mongrel panting at the leash. 'Hey, J.G., what's the hurry? Ain't I got time to douse my holy poker? It's got kinda red hot from all this riding.'

'Keep your big boy where it belongs — in your pants,' Anderson snapped back. 'You can have your fun time when we reach Caldwell.'

They had pulled into a small, rundown farm only ten miles from Wichita. After fifty miles hard riding their horses were on their last legs and showing it. So he had been glad to see that, as arranged, a shifty-looking southern horse dealer had fresh mounts awaiting them.

'They look like good uns,' he said, as they slung their saddles over them. After a quick mug of black coffee and paying the dealer, they had gone on their way again following a winding dust trail through pasture and woodland as the shades of night drew in and they eventually sighted the glowing lights of Wichita. They had taken the precaution of stuffing their civil war apparel into saddle-bags and folding the Confederate flag.

'First,' Anderson said, 'I'll book our tickets, then we'll load these mounts into the box car. The train leaves at midnight so we'll have time for some grub 'fore we hit. But, remember, I don't want anyone going AWOL' — he frowned at Josiah — 'we obey strict army discipline. In other words, leave the ladies alone for the time being.'

★   ★   ★

With his broken nose and gap-toothed grin, the bald and burly Sheriff Jim Clarke looked a bruiser. Instead of taming the town with his guns he was always ready to wade into a brawl with his fists. Of course, in extreme cases he might have to bring his Colt 'Thunderer' .41 into play. His finely-crafted Dickson three-barrel twelve gauge under his arm, Sheriff Jim emerged from the fug of tobacco, and lantern oil fumes, and the clamour of gamblers and dancing girls in Wichita's Grand Central saloon. He stood and surveyed the great bowl of stars above, sniffed at the prairie breeze that carried the steamy heat of cattle and horse dung from the corrals across the way. From the railroad came the clang and clatter of empty freight wagons being shunted into line ready to head south to Caldwell. All seemed peaceful.

Clarke was getting on in years. His bones had begun to creak like they needed oiling. Too many good dinners meant he had to breathe in deep when he buckled his belt these days. 'It's time I got myself a grubstake and got outa this game,' he muttered to himself. 'But how?'

Gone eleven. Time to get on with his rounds. He liked to be home at midnight. He peered through the steamed-up window of the Chung Lee chop-house. Looked like that bunch who rode in earlier, but they seemed to be behaving themselves. He climbed up the narrow stairs to Rosie's Rendezvous above and pushed through the beaded curtain.

★　★　★

'Hiya Shewiff.' Chinese Rosie, who had trouble pronouncing her 'r's, presided in her alcove bar. The oriental decor and quiet air indicated this to be a more upmarket premises than most of the town brothels. Her girls, in their silk dresses, were slim, neat and politely chatting at a row of small tables to their marks, encouraging them to buy yet another bottle of Rosie's California rosé, labelled 'Genuine Champagne'. The sheriff noted a couple of Wichita businessmen among their number. Poor saps.

'You sure on time for your weekly sweetener,' Rosie said, pushing an envelope over to him. 'Aincha?'

'You and your sisters of sin are donating to a good cause. It goes to the town council to help clean up the streets of this town and suchlike stuff. I get a small cut to cover my trouble.'

'I bet you do,' Rosie sang out.

'You get protection, doncha?' Clarke beamed at her as he tucked the envelope into his vest. 'It ain't just for me. I got my deputies to keep sweet, too.'

'Well, business not too good. Maybe me and ladies be movin' on soon.'

'Don't tell me where to,' Clarke sighed. 'Caldwell? Looks like Wichita'll soon be a back number.'

'So, why don' you spend some that money, twy Saigon Sue 'fore we go. The twicks she knows make your eyes water.'

'You joking? I wouldn't touch a scarlet woman with a broom pole.'

Clarke watched slim Sue usher her customer, swishing back a curtain, into her tiny room behind the table. 'Not me, Rosie. My old lady might have gone prematurely grey but I can assure you she's still frisky. She'll be ready and waitin' for me when I git back. We been married twenty-five years. We lead a

44

clean, God-fearin' life. But we have fun, too.'

'Nice,' Rosie sang out. 'In that case, so long Shewiff.'

★   ★   ★

'Come on, boys.' Down below Colonel Anderson paid for their chop suey, tossing a hefty tip on the table from stolen cash. He could afford to be generous. 'We've stuffed our bellies. Now we gotta go earn our pay.'

He led them ambling along the sidewalk to the Wells Fargo office on the corner. There were hardly any other folks around. He left Josiah Baines on watch and led the others around the back. They purloined two parked mustangs from the hitching rail as they did so, tied lariats to the saddle horns and hitched them to the barred window. When they set them charging off the whole frame tore loose from its bricks making them hightail it faster. Anderson, Mace Underwood, Skeeter

Hardy and Randy Sims clambered in first to locate the office safe and set to work. Whispering Rick remained on watch at the back. Following orders, Spotty Jed and Jawbone clambered upstairs to the telegraphist's office. Joyously, they smashed all the equipment. Then young Jed climbed from the window and reached out to a telegraph pole to cut all the wires. He started to climb on to the pitched roof.

'Where ya goin' now?' Jawbone called, but he had disappeared.

Downstairs Randy set his charges, boasting, 'This is gonna be a piece of cake,' as the others backed clear.

'Christ!' Jawbone cried, as the explosion cracked the upstairs floorboards. 'I'm gittin' out.'

Sheriff Clarke had left Rosie's and was walking back along the sidewalk when he heard the explosion. He, too, blasphemed. 'What'n hell was that?'

'Beats me,' Josiah Baines replied. He had spied the tin star on the big man's chest as he ran up. 'Something funny goin' on inside.' He pulled out his big revolver. 'You want any help?'

'Not just yet. Stand back. I'll handle this.' Clarke peered through the window at shadowy shapes amid the smoke and debris inside. He hammered on the locked door with the butt of his shotgun. 'This is the law. We got you surrounded. Throw down your guns and come out with your hands up.'

A smile flickered on Baines's thin lips and cadaverous face. His eyes sparkled with a strange light. He hungered to put a bullet into the fat fool's back; the stupid slob was asking for it. But he was mindful of Anderson's order to avoid needless killing. It seemed like the men in the noisy saloons were not yet aware of what was going on outside, so, as Clarke hammered at the door again, Josiah buffaloed him instead. The heavy blow of the revolver to the back of his neck felled the sheriff like a slaughtered ox.

'Come on,' Colonel Anderson yelled, handing the bag of cash to Mace and leading the men, all but Jed, out from the back of the bank at a run. 'We got a train to catch.'

Indeed, the mournful whistle of the midnight special was summoning late-comers. If they missed it they would be done for, so the robbers scampered away across the dusty street, past the corrals, to climb on to it. Anderson clambered on to the big locomotive's footplate as the huge stack began to shunt out steam smoke into the night air. He stuck his revolver into the engineer's face. 'Move it out,' he roared. 'Now!'

There were a few minutes to spare but the engineer decided not to argue with his uninvited guest, pulling on the controls as the stoker hurriedly fed the boiler flames.

There was only one passenger carriage, which the rest of the gang scrambled into as the rods jerked into motion and the wheels began to turn. The rest of the train was empty freight wagons rattling along in their wake.

'Where's Jed?' Mace asked.

'Hell knows,' Baines replied, and strode down the carriage checking the other passengers. Not many this time of night. Just a couple of travelling salesmen, a clutch of rowdy cowboys and two young ladies of the night who were obviously off in search of better pickings down at Caldwell.

At that moment Sheriff Clarke was coming round from the blow, groaning as he staggered to his feet. Suddenly he was flattened again as Spotty Jed lost his footing and landed on top of him hard.

'Ouf!' Clarke gasped. 'Who in tarnation are you?'

Jed had got his boot stuck trying to get down from the roof. In consternation, having seen his pals scatter for the station, he scrambled to his feet and kicked wildly at the man on the ground. Clarke caught his boot, twisted it, and threw him aside.

'Damn you.' Spotty Jed scrambled to his feet, jerked out his sixgun, his panicked fingers fumbling to cock the hammer as he aimed at the sheriff. 'You're a dead man, mister,' he screamed.

Still on the ground, Clarke's fingers had found the Dickson. He looked into the deathly hole of the youth's revolver and knew he had only one chance. He raised the shotgun and fired the first barrel, blasting Jed off his feet. He didn't need the other two. The boy lay on his back in the dust, blood leaking from a pattern of small shotholes in his chest beneath his shirt.

Clarke scrambled to his feet, kicked his gun away, knelt over him and demanded, 'Who are those guys? Where do they hang out? Tell me the truth and I'll get you outa this. Where's your hideout?'

'Go to hell.'

'Yeah?' Jim made the sign of the cross as the youth coughed his last. 'Looks like you'll be there first.'

The locomotive was slowly moving out as men tumbled out of the saloons.

Some were running across as the sheriff pointed the way, but a gang of cowboys leapt on to their ponies and, whooping and shooting, galloped across past the corrals to head off the train.

'Looks like we got a fight on our hands,' Mace yelled, leaning from the window, his first shot spinning one of them from the saddle. Jawbone, Randy, Amos, Skeeter and Whispering Rick took up other positions and joined in the fusillade.

'What's going on?' The cowboys on the train were getting to their feet. 'Who are you bunch?'

Josiah Baines's eyes were madly alight as he tugged on his forage cap and grinned. 'We are the re-formed Confederate army.' He levelled his New Model Colt at them, one hand ready to fan the hammer. 'You boys are Texans,' he drawled. 'So ahm gonna temper justice with mercy as some fool judge once said to me. Open that damn door and jump fer your lives.'

At first he thought they might argue,

but one led the way, swinging open the door and leaping out to hit the hard apron. The others quickly followed as Baines helped them on their way with his boot. 'As fer you missies.' He smiled at the screaming girls. 'Just shut up and sit tight. I'm gonna have fun with you.'

He strode back along the compartment and the two salesmen got the same treatment. One, however, was in such a hurry to comply as Baines booted him out, he slipped and tumbled under the wheels. His screams could be heard above the racket of the engine and the shooting. 'Aw, too bad,' Baines said.

The locomotive had yet to reach full thirty miles-an-hour speed and the cowboys were able to race alongside whooping and firing their guns to little avail as if it was carnival time, even though two more had been pitched from their stumbling mounts.

One in the lead had drunkenly lassoed the tall stack as if singlehand-edly he would haul the engine to a halt.

He was jerked from his pony and went flying along, his legs waving wildly, sparks crackling from the steel tobacco tin in his shirt breast pocket as he more or less ski'ed along on the flinty ground. He still hung on to the rope, looking up pleadingly at Colonel Anderson who leaned from the rattling cab alongside, reluctant or somehow unable to let go of the lariat.

'What the devil's that idiot playing at?' Anderson exclaimed, raising his revolver to take a potshot. At that point the cowboy gave up the chase, let go and slithered to a halt . . .

'Whoo-ee!' Randy exclaimed, as the cowboys fell back more interested in their crazy companion, pulling him to his feet and slapping his back. 'Did you ever see the likes of that? Saved by his tobacco tin. That galoot shoulda had his chest ripped apart.'

'Yeah,' Skeeter cackled. 'Some drunks are like cats. They got nine lives. The good god Bacchus looks after his own.'

They quietened down and, as the

train chugged on its way, tipped out the proceeds from the gunnysacks on to a seat and began the count. 'Boys,' Randy announed. 'We've excelled ourselves. I make it nearly seven thousand.'

The two young girls had crept up to gawp over their shoulders. 'Goodness,' one cried. 'I ain't never seen so much cash. Is it all yourn?'

'Too true, sweetheart,' Baines replied. 'So you jest keep your greedy eyes offen it. It ain't none of it fer you.'

'Aw, give 'em twenty dollars,' Mace grinned. 'Then they'll be nice to us.'

'What would Colonel Anderson say?' Josiah chided, threading his fingers into the curly mop of one of the girls and twisting her on her knees to the floor as the train reached top speed, smoke billowing, the rods reverberating. 'He don't believe in rewarding vice. An' I don' believe in payin' no whores. Go on, scream, sister. It's music to my ears. You boarded the wrong train tonight, the one the devil rides. Go on, git hold of that other bitch, boys. What yo' all hanging around fer?' He gave another whooping yell. 'Maybe we'll let 'em live, maybe we won't.' He grabbed his revolver and stuck it in the girl's ear. 'We don't believe in leaving witnesses. So it depends on you, sweetheart. You better try your bestest to please. And if you ever do tell anyone, like the sheriff, about this, or tell him what we look like, we'll be back to get you. You better believe that.'

4

'He's just a lad. Silly young fool.' Sheriff Clarke stared at Spotty Jed on the ground. 'I didn't wanna kill him. I had to. It was him or me. That's what comes of getting in with the wrong crowd. Aaw! He sure had a bad complexion!'

'Hey, look at that!'

'What?'

'Up there.' A storekeeper pointed to a turret atop the Wells Fargo building from which proudly fluttered in the breeze a Confederate flag. 'It's the Bonny Blue.'

'That,' Jim Clarke said, 'is adding insult to injury.' The parading of the flag was forbidden by law. 'So, that's what the kid was doing up there. Somebody better get it down.'

But the crowd which had gathered was in an angry mood. Most of the

56

folks were demanding their cash out of the bank. The manager had been sent for. He raised his hands and tried to appease them. 'We ain't got no cash left. Don't you people understand? It's all been stole.'

There was a hubbub of voices from the mob crowded around him. A widow who'd come running out in her nightdress screeched, 'My life savings! What am I going to do? I'll be destitute.'

She was on the verge of hysterics and the manager tried to console her. 'Don't panic! You'll all be reimbursed. Ours is a coast-to-coast company. But it will take time. We will need sworn testimonies from the sheriff and witnesses.'

'Why don't we go after 'em?' the town farrier urged. 'Sooner we catch up and swing them varmints from the nearest cottonwood the sooner we get our cash back.'

'Caldwell's only forty miles,' a cowboy shouted. 'If we set off now we could be there by sun-up. Those bastards killed three of my buddies. What are we waiting for?'

'Hang on!' Clarke shouted. 'I'm gonna set up a proper posse first thing in the morning. All able-bodied men are invited along. We'll have to go by horseback because there ain't another train until midday. Make sure you're well mounted and well armed.'

'Those guys ain't gonna hang around,' the cowhand whined, 'waiting for you to turn up.'

'In that case y'all better be prepared for a long ride even if it means goin' into the Nations after 'em. You heard the manager, I got a report to file, all kinda things to do like go and pick up them cowboy pals of yourn. And somebody's got the job of scraping up the remains of that salesman they kicked off the coach. He ain't a pretty sight. In fact, a mess of mincemeat might be the word. I sure ain't gonna get much sleep tonight. But I advise y'all to go back to your beds and let me handle this.'

When the crowd had dispersed Clarke led his deputies over to the track. 'Jeez,' one moaned, looking sick. 'How we s'posed to pick up that?'

'Hell, leave him,' the sheriff replied. 'Wild critters will soon clear up that mess. Just pick up them other three stiffs. Then we better try and git a bit of shut-eye.'

*　*　*

Colonel Anderson ordered the engineer to halt the big locomotive a few miles out of Caldwell. When the guard from the calaboose at the rear end of the freight wagons came running along the track to see what was going on Anderson stuck his Remington up his nose and drawled, 'Come and jine us.'

Josiah Baines was in favour of killing the railroad men out of hand, but Anderson told his boys to hogtie them tight. 'How many times I gotta tell you, Josiah, we treat prisoners-of-war with respect? We only dispose of armed combatants out to get us.'

'Yeah,' Josiah growled, 'and one day that could well be our downfall.'

They lowered the ramps and dragged their whinnying horses out of the vans, leaping aboard and riding on their way into town. But there they encountered a problem. Randy had run out of dynamite. In the early hours of the morning they stood in Caldwell's deserted main street outside the bank.

'There's no point in breaking in there if we can't blow the safe,' Colonel Anderson hissed in exasperation. 'Come on, we will head on. There could well be a posse after us.'

Although Baines's ardour had been doused and he had no reason to hang around he let the others ride on ahead. He crossed the street to a shuttered general store, glanced around, smashed a window with his elbow, reached inside and unlocked the door. Inside, he struck a match on his revolver butt, cupped it and found the till. He pulled his skinning knife and forced it open, helping himself to a wad of dollars and gold coins. 'Not a bad haul,' he whispered.

Suddenly a lantern was lit upstairs, casting light. There was the sound of voices and footsteps creaked the staircase. The storekeeper had a gun in his hand. 'Who's there?' he quavered.

Baines smiled and stepped back behind the door, peering through the crack as a pair of bony legs beneath a nightshirt appeared. When a bald-headed man stepped through into the darkened store Baines curved a wiry arm around his face. Blood spurted as Baines slit the man's jugular.

'Henry,' a woman screeched. 'Are you all right?'

She, too, descended warily and Baines caught her by the throat, pricking his knife to it and hugging her to him. She was a tubby little body, her warmth arousing him.

'Who else you got here?'

'Please, sir, only my children. Don't

kill us all.' She stared with horror at her husband's body on the boards in its dark pool of blood.

'Waal, that depends on you, don't it? Git back up them stairs and back into bed, lady. You found yourself a new rooster. You gonna ride with Satan tonight.'

When he was done with her he tore up a sheet and bound her wrists and ankles to the brass bedposts and gagged her.

Baines met her pleading eyes, scratching his razor-sharp blade down her naked body from gizzard to gut, leaving a thin, zig-zagging red line. 'Ah want to thank you, ma'am. As you see ahm a true southern gentleman and am sparing your life. Ye'll be fine jest as long as too much blood don't trickle outa ya 'fore they find ya. So, I'll say so long.'

Calmly, he left the store, helping himself to some barley sugar on the way, swung on to his mustang and set off at a gallop after his companions. A full moon soared high and he cackled with satisfaction. Not far now to the Nations. Nobody would ever find them.

★ ★ ★

That, for the time being would prove to be the case. Shortly after sun-up Sheriff Jim Clarke convened a posse of fifty-two men and led them in pursuit, only pausing *en route* to pick up two torn and tattered *filles de joie* who had been tossed from the train and who had tumbled down into a ravine. When the posse reached Caldwell they found that the general store had been robbed, its owner murdered and his wife raped. Her children's screams had brought help before she had lost too much blood from the knife scar which seemed to read 'Josiah'. As a reminder of her experience, it would stay with her the rest of her life.

'I'd say she's lucky to be alive,' Sheriff Clarke commented gruffly. 'Sounds to me like that feller who was outside Wells Fargo at Wichita.'

He didn't say much more because a reporter from the local rag was listening. Clarke already felt a fool from the way he had been tricked. He would certainly never forget that gaunt face, the heavy moustache, the forage cap pulled down over one eye; a slim-hipped *hombre* in his forties but with the swagger of a young stud. For some reason it gave him a chill down his spine.

The posse set off again mid-morning, Clarke at their head. He planned to cross over into the Indian Nations and check out the small towns of Ponca City, Powhuska and Pawnee. But, in truth, he had little idea of where the raiders might be. They could have headed on along the panhandle into what was known as No Man's Territory, a regular haunt of outlaws and no-goods. It was badlands country cut through by ravines and black mesas. Or they might be planning to cross the Cinnamon and Canadian rivers and strike south-west across the plains to Old Greer county and maybe on back into Texas. Or they could have verged south-west down past the Great Cherokee Lake or east into Arkansas. 'They coulda gone any which-a-way,' he muttered as he rode.

★ ★ ★

'*Bonne santé*, gentlemen.' Colonel John Anderson had attired himself in his bullet-holed grey frockcoat, with yellow collar of his cavalry brigade, and yellow Austrian braid insignia of rank on his sleeves. He often used the mongrel French still spoken by some in his home state. He raised his bottle in a toast. 'Here's to the Rebel Raiders. You all did well, obeyed your orders to the letter but for poor Spotty Jed. He disobeyed and suffered the consequences. However, it was a noble gesture. Here's to his memory.'

Josiah Baines had decked himself out in his old uniform, tight cavalry pants with the yellow stripes up the sides, pea jacket with sergeant's chevrons, his cap perched at a saucy angle on his convict-cropped head, his lips, as always, half-smiling beneath his heavy moustache. 'We hit them banks so hard and fast they didn't know if we'd come or gawn,' he said, pointing to the stacks of notes and coins on the roulette table before them. 'I make our tally $3,930 dollars from Eureka, $420 from Eldorado, $7,000 in gold and greenbacks from Wichita, and my measly $150 from that store in Caldwell, making a grand total of $11,500.'

'If we hadn't run out of dynamite at Caldwell,' Anderson said, frowning at Randy Sims, 'we could have hit the jackpot there, too.'

'If that storekeeper hadn't come down in his nightshirt to see what I was up to I needn't have had to slit his throat.' Baines smiled, relishing the memory. 'Damn fool. I shoulda done his wife in, too.'

'I don't think that was necessary, Josiah,' Anderson replied, icily. 'But I'll overlook it. You did well, boys. So, fair shares for all.'

He swiftly counted out a thousand dollars for each of the six men, passing it across the green baize of the rickety roulette table. 'Don't thank me. You have earned it.'

'Hang on,' Randy whined, with his Jewish Bronx twang. 'What's this? What about the four and a half thou' left after you've had your share?'

'That, my friend, goes into our war chest to support our noble cause.'

'Yeah, well, I was born in Noo York and the only noble cause I support is my own. You'd have got very little of this if it weren't for my skills. I'm a top cracksman. My agreement was for top dollar. What skills have you numbskulls got, apart from killin'? So you better hand over another thousand to me pretty sharp, Colonel, or I'm out.'

Anderson stroked his goatee and twirled his moustachios, holding Randy's gaze while he considered this. '*Who* is the leader of this outfit? *I* decide this. So all I can suggest, Mr Sims, is be grateful for what you get.'

'Or get out,' Baines drawled. 'You better remember, lardgut, you couldn't have pulled off any of these jobs without the colonel's organizing skills and our firepower. So I suggest you shut your mouth.'

'Too true,' Skeeter Hardy, in his worn Army of Tennessee uniform, growled. 'You think we're gonna give some jumped-up bluebelly more'n us?'

Mace's fingers were hovering over the grip of his revolver, and Skeeter looked ready to go for the knife stuck in his belt. Randy Sims's Adam's apple bobbed in his chubby throat as he shifted in his seat. But Anderson stepped in. 'No need for this, boys. I'm sure Sims understands our reasoning. He's free to get out if he wants, with his share.'

Jawbone gave a guffaw and slapped the little New Yorker on his pudgy back. 'Not sure I'd like to bet on how far you'd get, pal.'

'Nor me,' whispered Rick. 'That's being greedy, that is.'

'All right, boys, you win.' Randy quickly pocketed his thousand. 'It ain't what was agreed but I'm willing to go along.'

'Yeah.' Mace tugged his daddy's old campaign hat down over his eyes with a snarling threat. 'You better be.'

Mind you, Mace wasn't sure just what the colonel planned to do for the noble cause with all that extra cash, but that was up to him.

'So, what's the next move?' Randy enquired.

'The next move,' Josiah replied, standing up and giving the roulette wheel a twirl, 'is for me to start winning back all that nice moolah you got.'

Their venue could not be called a saloon. Alcohol was strictly banned in the Indian Nations. But since the war the wilderness had become a haven for ex-soldiers, killers, rapists, thieves and just general drifters on the lam. The few federal deputy marshals who tried to police the vast territory from Fort Smith, in the adjacent state of Arkansas, had a hard job even catching whiskey peddlers who slipped in across the border.

No, this was just a log cabin in Ponca City in which Ponca Bob, as he was known, sold whatever hooch he had and presided over the faded roulette table, his prized possession.

'Right, you can unbolt the door now, Bob, and let them other layabouts in.' Anderson pressed a gold double eagle into his hand. 'As long as they ain't blacks or savages or' — he glared at Randy Sims — 'or Jews. No offence, but we don't want no trouble tonight. Just keep that barleycorn flowing. Our business meeting is concluded, boys. Time to relax.'

'Jeez,' Randy hissed through his teeth. 'You southerners are something else. You ain't prejudiced by any chance?'

'No.' Jawbone jumped up with a whoop to brandish a fistful of dollars.

'But we got one troublesome Jew in here already and that's as many as we can handle.'

Like many Indians in the Nations, Ponca Bob was in half-native, half-whiteman get-up, white collarless shirt, waistcoat, fringed leather britches, moccasins and a headband holding back his long black hair from his monolithic features. He frowned at the Raiders, nodded, and unbolted the wooden door after checking through a small grille who was outside.

A big-bearded settler shoved through, shouting, 'What you locked up for, Bob? I got me a terrible thirst. What you playing at? Counting your cash?'

'Don't try jumping the queue, fungus-face,' young Mace growled. 'We're first.'

'Holy Moses!' the big man boomed. 'What's this, a fancy dress ball? Or is the war on again?'

'You could say so,' Anderson replied. 'But, my friend, 'tis best not to jest about matters you know nothing of.

Perhaps I should stress that when we are gone you forget about us.'

Ponca Bob had let another settler in, German by the sound of him, but had raised his palm, shaking his head at two Indians and bolted the door on them.

'We sure got some rare birds roosting here tonight,' the black-bearded one muttered to the German farmer as they eagerly watched Bob turn a spigot of a barrel and the precious copper-coloured spirit trickled out into his jug.

'Dollar one shot.' Bob lined up a row of clay mugs and tipped a portion of whiskey into each. 'It me go jail.'

'Sure, keep it coming.' Mace slapped silver dollars down. 'If there ain't no white wimmin in this township available, how's about you rustle us up a coupla squaws? We ain't prejudiced, eh, boys?'

Jawbone gave a howl of mirth and stamped out a war dance on the dirt floor. 'Just as long as they got their bits an' pieces in the right places it's all the same to us.'

Ponca Bob nodded, impassively. 'Maybe.'

The big bearded man beamed. 'Looks like it's gonna be quite a night, don't it? Somebody seems to have won the lottery.'

5

In the not far off future the big, saucepan-shaped Indian Territory would be opened up to massive land-runs and become known as Oklahoma. Already there was considerable agitation to allow white settlers access to these fine lands. In the bitterness of the war and its aftermath of Reconstruction, the Indian tribes, whether they supported the Union or not, had been treated shabbily, many of their tribal self-governing rights snatched from them and the land had become a dumping ground for remnants of native peoples who had survived the genocide from all parts of the States. The white tide moving west was forbidden access to this promising land. But a few of the emigrants defied the law and sneaked in, grabbing a few acres, ploughing, sowing, building cabins and 'soddy' schools for their children. Such a settlement was Ponca City, a huddle of cabins, false fronts and a trade store where the few whites existed side by side with the majority native people.

But if the birds had been in Ponca City by the time Jim Clarke and his posse arrived they had flown. It was the same at other small Indian townships. Colonel Anderson and his hearties? Never heard of them. The Kansans had come up against the intransigence of the native population. Before the war many of the Cherokee had taken to white-men's ways, raising crops, trading far and wide. But many had chosen to fight on the side of the Confederacy in the great conflict mainly to hang on to their own black slaves. They had suffered badly in the aftermath for so doing. Few now trusted any white man and there was a wall of silence.

The posse rode deep south through Stillwater, crossing the Cimarron until they reached Fort Reno in the centre of the Nations. 'Most of our forces have been sent south to fight the Apache,' the captain there told Clarke. 'All I've got are fifty men to patrol the whole of this western sector. You think I've got time to go looking for a bunch of Kansan bank robbers?'

By now most of the possemen had lost their enthusiasm. Many were shopkeepers or farmers unused to hard riding. 'We ain't getting nowhere,' the farrier complained. 'I got a business to run. I vote we head home.'

This caused some argument for a few of the more pugilistic members had counted on being in at the kill after the chase and wanted to see justice done. Clarke took a show of hands and, after staying the night in the Reno stockade, led the disconsolate force back north towards Kansas.

* * *

For Cassius Clacy it was good to be finally out on the trail, although he was by no means sure what good he could do now. But the early spring sunshine filled him with optimism as he put his mustang to a hard lope. At Eldorado he made his enquiries, heard their sad story, and visited the lady in her rooms above her hat shop. The doc had got the bullet out from her shoulder and gave her a fifty-fifty chance of recovery. She looked up at him from her sick bed and lisped out, 'Get him for me, Sheriff. Mad dogs got to be put down.'

No reason to point out that he was a deputy with only six months' experience of law-upholding under his belt. Before that he'd spent his life herding cattle or selling melons off the back off his daddy's wagon down in San Antonio. 'I'll do what I can, ma'am,' he promised.

It seemed like the only figures who stood out were the white-haired colonel and that lean, mean side-kick who had a taste for humiliating women. Mary's bird's-eye view as she perched on the rooftop was as good a description of the raiders as he had. In all it didn't amount to much.

The general consensus was that they had taken the Wichita trail and Cass urged his mount on. A huge black and viridian mushroom cloud had blown up over the plain as if portending doom to mankind. It filled the young Texan with doubts about the point of this expedition, but he followed the winding trail up hill and down dale heading for the clear sky beyond the dark cloud. With about fifty miles under his belt the mustang was blowing hard and Cass eased him to a walk. There was another ten or so to go to Wichita and he didn't think the pony would make it. Maybe he should sleep out tonight?

He was no great tracker, but as he passed one of the few and far-between farmhouses he saw the prints of about half-a-dozen riders' hoofprints veering through damp clay into its entranceway. Funny.

Cass slipped from the saddle, left the mustang to graze by the trailside, and made his way through some willows to the back of tumbledown shacks. Smoke was trickling from a chimney. There were a half-dozen horses in a corral and a fine Palomino mare prancing around whinnying at them from an adjacent fenced-off field. Her hide glowed the colour of newly minted gold and she tossed her blonde mane and tail proudly. It was love at first sight for Cass — and probably for some of those mustangs, too. 'Jeez,' he murmured. 'Fancy owning a hoss like that.'

Just then the cabin door banged open and a man walked over to the corral swinging a bucket. He was a scruffy individual in a floppy-brimmed hat and dishevelled clothes. He leaned over the fence and started feeding the mustangs handfuls of split corn.

Cass crept out of the woods and up close, jamming his Never Miss into his spine. 'Hold it right there, mister.'

The man froze. 'Whadja want?'

'You're under arrest.'

'What for?'

'Put your wrists behind your back. Drop the bucket, nice and slow now.'

He cuffed him with the irons he had brought from his saddle-bag. 'I'm the deputy sheriff from Eureka and I have good reason to believe you are in cahoots with the Anderson gang.'

'Get lost. Never heard of 'em.'

'You will be charged with bank robbery and several counts of homicide. I am pretty certain the gang changed horses here, didn't they?'

The ferrety-eyed individual turned to face him. 'I don't know what you're talking about. I'm an honest horse dealer.'

'I ain't never heard of such a breed. There ain't no such thang as an honest one. Anyhow, I'm taking you in. Only hope I can keep them folks back at Eldorado and Eureka from lynching you. They're mightily riled-up.'

Cass glanced back at the cabin in case the fellow had any associates but all looked quiet. 'My own boss, Marshal Brady, generally leaves his key under the mat outside the jailhouse. Funny habit that of his. Anybody could get in.

Like a lynch mob.'

'Aw, come off it,' the dealer whined. 'They just asked me to wait for 'em here with some fresh mounts. I don't know nuthin' about no killings.'

'That ain't how it is in law. You're an accomplice. I'd better read you your rights.'

'Come on, pal,' the man wheedled. 'Gimme a break.'

It was odd how the thought of a hempen necktie made men jittery. Cass guessed he'd got him hooked. 'Waal,' the Texan drawled. 'I wanna go on after those guys. Tell you what. I'll trade you for that Palomino over yonder. I'll give you my nice li'l mustang I left down the lane. How about that for fair exchange?'

'You're joking,' the dealer protested. 'That's a two-hundred dollar horse. A thoroughbred four-year-old Spanish mount.'

'You don't want to? Right, we'd better head back to Eureka.'

'Hang on. You mean you'll forget you ever saw me?'

'Sure. You're just an honest dealer. Give me a receipt for the deal. That's the last you'll hear about it.'

'You twisting sonuvabitch!'

'You wanna saddle her up?'

'It's that or Eureka?' The dealer gave him a poisonous look. 'Yeah, sure.'

* * *

'Wow!' Cassius gave a whoop of delight as he slung his leg over the seventeen-hands-tall mare. 'Steady, baby,' he urged, holding tight to the reins as she zig-zagged away along the trail. 'You an' me gonna be pals. You wanna go? Right, let's go.' And he gave the big horse her head as she tore away into a gallop. 'Go, baby, go,' he yelled. 'Whee-hoo!' He rode standing in the stirrups, the wind rippling her mane into his face as he leaned forward over her neck, shouting in her ear. It was at least two miles before she slowed. 'Yeah, you sure can go, cain't ya?' he crooned, settling deep in the saddle as he put her to a steady lope, eating up the miles, coming out into a blaze of sunset from beneath the black cloud. And before long, as darkness closed in, the lights of Wichita appeared not far off on the plain.

* * *

'You're a bit late, aincha?' The 'keep in the Grand Central saloon in Wichita eyed the young deputy sheriff in his low-crowned Stetson, a tin star pinned to the tweed waistcoat buttoned tight around his wool-shirted chest as he ambled in, spurs clinking on his dusty boots. 'The posse from here set off ages ago.'

'Got kinda held up.' Cass thirstily licked his dry lips as he watched the barman flick the foam head from a glass of beer with his spatula. He caught it as it was slid along to him. 'Looks like I missed the action.'

It was good to be back in the rumbustious cattle town which he had first encountered after a long haul up the Chisholm trail from San Antonio, Texas. He had been one of the hands driving a herd of a thousand longhorns up through Fort Worth, fighting through droughts, lightning storms, crossing the mighty Red River in flood, hitting back attacks by hostile Indians as they crossed the Nations, and finally reaching the Kansan railheads.

It had been an experience that made men of boys, but not one he was over eager to repeat. So, reluctant to return to Texas, when he had been offered a position of deputy lawman along at Eureka he had jumped at the chance. Now he was not so sure. To tell the truth he had had his fill of being ordered around like some office boy by Brady. And, it had to be admitted, Mary had become a problem. Maybe it might be best to go and keep on going.

The trouble was he had had his own life savings, some sixty dollars, in the Eureka bank, too. That was now in the pocket of Anderson or his cronies. Brady had refused to advance him a loan on next month's wages to go after them. What did he think he was going to live on — air? He had paid a dollar at the livery for stall and feed for the Palomino overnight. She was too good to leave out on the street. By the time he had paid for his beer and some grub he would have about eight dollars left. 'Aw, hell,' he groaned, and went across to join in a card game.

An hour later he was ten dollars better off and decided to quit while he was ahead. At least he could have a couple more beers and enjoy the lively scene. He even paid a few cents for a whirl with one of the dancing girls. He was back at the bar when amid all the din he heard a raucous screech behind him. Maggie McGinty was prodding him with the point of her parasol.

'What you doing here, Deputy? Come to arrest me? You think I jumped my bail? I wouldn't do that. Why doncha give a gal a chance?'

'Quit pokin' me, you demon. I ain't interested in you. I got other fish to fry.

I'm after them bank robbers.'

'Who-whee! You gonna capture 'em all by your manly self? What are you, suicidal?'

'Yeah.' He shrugged. 'I guess I must be to be a deputy. To tell the truth I just been thinking about maybe going back to poking cows.'

'Why don't you poke me, instead? Help a gal raise her fine.' In her somewhat shop-soiled scarlet dress Maggie was as skinny as a boy. Her horribly-dyed yellow hair radiated from her head like a halo and she gave him a cheeky smile. 'You could at least buy me a drink.'

'Sorry,' Cass sighed. 'I'm practically skint. I can't afford you. Not that I would if I could. I'm gonna bed down with Guinevere.'

'Who's she?'

'She's beautiful. My new horse.'

'What sorta name is that?'

'She was the queen of King Arthur. You know, knights of old. She two-timed him with some guy called Lancelot.'

'Tell me something new. Hey, Charlie.' She beckoned to the barkeep. 'Give us a bottle of Knock 'Em Dead. Come on, Deputy. It's my treat. Drink up. Quit looking so mournful. Marshal Brady's a long way away. So's that lady friend of yourn. Don't look so surprised. She ain't the best kept secret in Eureka. Her husband's the only one who don't seem to know.'

'You're crazy,' Cass muttered.

'What? Has she made you vow to live like a monk while you're away? You can bet she's cuddled up with her hubby right now. Wouldn't you say that's kinda hypocritical?'

'Waal, I guess she has to — '

'While you're not allowed to. These holier than holy wimmin they make me sick.'

'She ain't like that.'

By the time they had killed the bottle, the saloon had emptied and Maggie caught hold of his arm. 'Cass, I git lonely this time of night. I got a room upstairs. For you it's half-price.'

Well, how could he refuse in his fuddled state? It wouldn't have been gentlemanly. So, a tad unsteadily, he headed up the stairs with her. It had to be better than bedding down with his horse.

The saloon was being opened in the early morning as he left Maggie. The bony lady was sleeping naked, but for her crumpled stockings, beneath the blanket. Cass tucked a greenback dollar in her garter — the going price — and muttered, 'So long.' She flickered her eyelashes, murmuring, 'Yeah, see ya around.'

A couple of pickled eggs from the jar on the bar and a beer set him up. He sauntered along Main Street to saddle his Palomino and went clipping out of town beneath great billows of pink-tinged clouds that rolled across the clear blue heaven above.

6

Cass followed the rail line south to Caldwell and headed on across the prairie. He squinted into the sun from beneath the curly brim of his battered Stetson as he saw the fifty-strong posse kicking up dust, thundering towards him.

'Howdy, boys,' he yelled, as the riders slowed to a halt. 'You given up the chase? Aincha had no luck?'

'What's that to you?' one of the disgruntled men growled. 'Where've *you* been hidin'?'

'Well, I'll be danged,' Sheriff Clarke barked out. 'If it ain't that wanderin' Texan cowboy, Cassius Clacy. What you doing here, son?'

'I'm going after Colonel Anderson and his gang.'

'What? You gonna arrest 'em all by yourself?' another of the men jeered, amid laughter. 'Going after 'em on that fancy horse?'

'Waal,' Cass drawled. 'It ain't exactly my idea. But I'm following orders. Howdy, Mr Clarke. How ya been?'

'What? Is Brady trying to get you killed?' The sheriff beamed. 'Where is he? Keeping his backside warm in an armchair back in Eureka? How's he been treating you, Cass?'

'Well, we don't exactly see eye to eye, but he's OK. They hit the Eureka bank first so I'm on the case, Sheriff.'

'How come Brady's sent you? Bill Molineux's his senior man.'

'Bill's outa action for a bit. He got shot in the thigh. So I got this chance.'

'Huh! Some chance! You think you can gun-down seven hardened criminals with that five-shot of yourn? That .38's a farce as a manstopper. You must know that yourself.'

'Aw, it's a handy li'l piece.' Cass gave them all his big, dare-devil grin, although he felt far from confident about things. 'I got my Creedmore rifle, too.'

The men guffawed at his optimism and Sheriff Clarke pulled out his big .41 Thunderer. 'This is the gun you need. It'll put any man in his grave.' He fired a shot into the air, making his mustang prance. 'A real rip-roarer, huh?'

'Yeah, and it's got a kick worse than a horse, over-penetrates and ricochets badly. Not for me, Mr Clarke.'

'So, now you're an expert on firearms?' Jim laughed in his deep barrel-chested way. 'This kid was just a raw cowhand up on the trail when I first bumped into him six months ago. He helped me out in a barfight. I'll admit he's got a handy right. I knew Brady was in need of a new deputy so I sent him along to Eureka with a letter of commendation. He seems to have gone up in the world.'

'Sure,' one of Jim's own deputies snarled. 'In his own estimation.'

'I'm doing OK,' Cass protested, and grinned at Jim. 'Thanks to you. Waal, I better be after them bad boys.'

'Hold it right there,' the sheriff told him, sticking his Colt away. 'I got something to discuss with you before you head off on some wild goose chase.'

He gave a jerk of his head for Cass to join him out of earshot. 'Just what you planning to do?'

'Waal.' Cass figured he had already crossed the line into the Nations. He didn't want to go back without at least trying. 'Marshal Brady told me to infiltrate. Get in with this gang, let him know their moves and if they come back into Kansas he'd be ready for 'em.'

'Marshal?' Clarke gave a scoffing laugh. 'He's no more a federal marshal than I am. Infiltrate? You think you're just gonna ride into this vast wilderness, find those guys and they'll welcome you with open arms? You're living in cloud cuckoo land, Cass. That don't make a speck of sense.'

The younger man shrugged. 'Maybe . . . '

Jim's watery-grey eyes held his gaze and he gritted out, 'There's a lot of bounty building up on these characters, a thousand on Anderson's head alone. You interested in being my partner?' He lowered his voice. 'We'll rake through every possible hideout. And when we find 'em we'll take 'em.'

'Sounds fine to me, Jim. I only got one problem. I'm more or less broke.'

'Don't you worry about that, boy.' The sheriff's eyes twinkled. 'I'll grubstake ya. You can repay me when the rewards start coming in. We'll forget about being lawmen. Bounty hunters we'll be.'

He winked and turned his mustang back to the posse. 'I'm taking a month's leave of absence. Me and Cass are going to sniff around, see if we can put anything up. We may do better on our own.'

'What am I s'posed to tell the mayor?' Zach Stevens, one of his deputies, cried. 'You cain't just walk out.'

'If I'm not back in a month they might want to make you sheriff.

Meantime, Zach, you can take care of things in Wichita. Can you tell my wife? She'll understand.'

There were puzzled shouts of protest from some of the mob, but Clarke ignored them and grabbed one of the pack-mules. 'I'll take Lop Ears along.'

He gave a wave and cantered away from them in the direction of Ponca City and the westering sun, Clacy, on his sprightly Palomino, trotting alongside.

'He's got a nerve,' Zach said. 'He thinks he can make hisself some cash. Mind you, he's the sort of guy who might.'

'He ain't got a chance,' his fellow deputy opined. 'All he'll find is a lonesome grave.'

*　*　*

The sun was like a burning coal sliding away down the far side of the world as they spied the cabins and false fronts of Ponca City through the trees.

Back in Wichita before he left, a newsboy had been shouting, 'Murder! Rape! Robbery!'

'You better see this.' Cass dug a crumpled copy of the *Bugle* from his saddle-bag. The banner headline reflected the gory news: REB RAIDERS STRIKE TERROR ACROSS SOUTH KANSAS.

Jim Clarke pulled in his mustang and studied the front-page report. *''Ten men slaughtered in gunfights. A young outlaw killed by our own Sheriff Jim Clarke. He has led out a posse from Wichita in pursuit of the gang','* he muttered. *''Four women raped or sexually molested'.'* They must have got the line mended and got a message through about what happened on the train and in Caldwell. *''Riotous scenes outside the banks . . . .''*

He made a downturned grimace. 'Hang on to this. It'll come in handy to light fires. And you better put your tin badge outa sight. Damn newspaper reporters! Bounty hunters will be prowling like vultures after carrion when they read this. We're gonna have to act fast.'

'Trouble is,' Cass pointed out, 'we don't really know what these guys look like, apart from the white-haired colonel.'

'There's the slim-hipped character with the heavy moustache. I won't forget *his* face in a hurry. Sounds like he was the one who raped the storekeeper's wife and led the fun and games on the train.'

Cass put in, 'The girls said there was one little fat one who didn't join in the activities. Identified by the bank staff as the safe-blower.'

'That's right.'

'Otherwise, there was a young one in a Confederate campaign hat,' Cass recalled, 'and an older man addressed as Skeeter and two others who could be any kind of riffraff.'

'All with strong southern speech, like yourn,' Clarke reminded him. 'Anderson originates from Louisiana so that figures.'

'I ain't from Louisiana,' Cass protested. 'I'm from Texas. They're different from us.'

'Yeah, well, we'll head in and take a look. My information is there's a bootlegger operates from a cabin in this township.'

Woodsmoke wafted from the chimneys of the murky stores and cabins as the occupants battened down their shutters and prepared their suppers. There were no street lights and few people out as they rode in on the hard mud mainstreet.

Jim nosed his mustang and the mule up an alleyway, Cass following on his Palomino, its white mane and tail doffing, and in the half-darkness they saw two Indians in a drunken stupor sprawled outside a cabin. 'It kinda advertises what they sell inside,' Clarke said, stepping down, pulling his shotgun from the boot and hammering with its butt on the cabin door.

One of the Indians had staggered to his feet to peer curiously at the

Palomino and, as Cass followed the sheriff, the other on the ground grabbed at his leg, obviously begging for baccy or booze.

Cass kicked him off and growled at the other, 'You leave that hoss alone.'

A grille had slid open in the locked door and Ponca Bob's worried face regarded them. 'We closed,' he said.

'It's OK,' Clarke shouted, poking his shotgun barrel through the grille to prevent it closing. 'We ain't marshals. No need to worry about that. All we want is some vittles and maybe a drink.'

'No booze here. Against law,' Bob said. 'Wait.' He managed to slide the grille closed.'

'They ain't very welcoming,' Cass said. 'Must think we're after them. It's gone quiet in there. What they up to?'

He strode back to hitch the Palomino to the rail and whipped his rifle out to prod into the drunken Indian's face. 'I said to keep your hands off her. I ain't gonna tell you again.'

The man slurred some remark and

pushed the rifle away, laughing in his face and falling over again.

Inside, Ponca Bob had hurriedly rolled his whiskey barrel into an alcove and covered it with a plank and some rags, then surlily unbolted the door and allowed them in. 'All we got venison stew.'

The whiff of whiskey fumes mingled with those of tobacco smoked by a bunch of hard-eyed white men who stood around the roulette table. There was, too, the gamey scent from the contents of a cauldron which had probably been bubbling on the stove for a week or two.

Another white man in dirty range clothes was sprawled on a couch of furs, an arm around an Indian woman. 'What in tarnation do you want, Sheriff?' he growled.

Clarke recognized him as a no-good named Ed Collins, who hung around Wichita. 'Possibly the same as you,' he said. 'And I ain't talking whiskey and whores.'

'Hoo! Listen to big white man,' the squaw squawked.

A broad-chested bearded man was standing by a makeshift plank bar. 'Good evening, gentlemen. Welcome to our little gathering. Yes, we all know who you are, Mr Clarke. We saw you ride in at the head of your fine posse the other day. Be assured there's no ill-feeling towards you here.'

'There's no need for none,' Clarke replied, tipping a ladle into the soup and filling two wooden bowls Ponca Bill handed him.

'That a dollar,' the Ponca said.

'Most appetizing,' the sheriff remarked, as they found barrels to sit at a rickety table in the corner, keeping their rifle and shotgun within reach.

'Yeah,' Cass agreed, as he chewed on a slice of overcooked venison. 'Very tasty. Hope it don't give me the runs.'

'Just so you boys understand,' Clarke announced through a mouthful. 'we're here on private business.'

'Once a lawman allus a lawman.' The

slurred remark came from Jawbone, who was standing beside the roulette table as if expecting trouble. His shirt sleeves had been torn away at the armpits to display his muscular arms, a headband held back his greasy long hair, and his black eyes smouldered in dark hollows. He fingered a long-barrelled revolver laid on the table. 'Just what kinda business you figure you're in *now*, pal?'

Clarke carefully picked up his shot-gun as he rose to face the challenge in his eyes. 'Could say I'm a hunter.'

'Just what you hunting?' A man on the far side of the roulette wheel, possibly his sidekick, posed the question in a husky, whispered tone. Both his hands were out-stretched on the table but an ivory-handled revolver on each hip was not far from reach.

'Maybe the most treacherous, murder-ing, lying, raping, two-timing, cruellest critters who roam the Territory.'

The bearded onlooker laughed ner-vously as he backed away towards a

101

wall, although there was no escape from a scattergun in such small confines as the cabin. 'Sounds to me like you're describing the Anderson gang.'

'You guessed it. You interested in 'em, too?'

'Oh, no, I'm just a settler. Got a small patch up the road. If I had seen those fellers — which I haven't — I wouldn't breathe a word. I got a wife and six kids. It would be more than my life would be worth. I better be getting home.'

'Stay where you are,' Jim growled, thumbing back his first hammer.

'Even if I knew where they'd gone — which I don't — I wouldn't tell you . . . '

'Ha!' Ed Collins, reclining on the furs, guffawed. 'He's scared shitless.'

'Waal, *I* ain't.' Jawbone's drawl pegged him as hailing from Arkansas or even further south. 'An' I don't take kindly to words about Colonel Anderson and his boys. I ain't got nuthin' aginst 'em. Good southern boys. They jest rightin' a few wrongs.'

'That's one way of putting it.' Cass pushed his bowl aside and stretched his arms as he stood. 'My daddy fought for the south. Lost a leg in Antietam's breeches.'

'Maybe he shoulda kept his leg in his own britches,' Ed jeered, but nobody appreciated the pun.

'He died from blood pizen,' Cass went on. 'My mammy was left to run the farm. She died soon after of grief or damn hard work. I can understand how those boys feel. The war ain't yet over for a lot of 'em. Me? All I feel is gut hatred whenever I see that Yankee flag.'

There was silence while they contemplated him. 'Aw, hell,' he said. 'Any place here I can stable my horse?'

'Stable out back.' Bob jerked a thumb. 'One dollar.'

'And how about a sup of whiskey? I can kinda smell it on the breath of y'all.'

'No whiskey here,' Bob said. 'All gone.'

Cass's interruption had defused what had been a tense face-off. Jim Clarke wasn't sure what Cass was up to, but neither was he sure who these two hard men were. They might well be fellow bounty hunters. So he lowered the three-barrelled Dickson and growled, 'Yeah, that's a likely story. Come on, cough it up, Bob.'

Jawbone and Whispering Rick, for it was they, appeared to have relaxed, so Clarke strode behind the bar and kicked the plank away. 'Aha, what's this?'

Bob eyed him, plaintively. 'You not sheriff no more?'

'No. I'm just a weary traveller. All I want is a sup of the hard stuff. Mind you, I don't agree with it being sold to Indians. They cain't handle it. Sends 'em crazy. But, hell, I ain't opposed to selling it to white men.'

As Bob rolled out the barrel, Jawbone jerked his head at Whispering Rick, grabbed his jacket, and they made their way out of the cabin, slamming the door.

Ponca Bob lined up four mugs of the evil brew on the plank bar. 'One dollar shot.'

'What is this,' Jim asked. 'A dollar house?' He jerked out his Colt and blasted a bullet into the sod ceiling, showering them with bits of dried mud. 'Ponca Bob, I'm arresting you for running moonshine. Ye'll get two years down the river for this.'

Bob froze, and the blood seemed to drain from his dark cheeks.

Jim roared with laughter and stuffed the gun back in his holster. He slapped the Indian's shoulder. 'You look like a paleface now. Only joking, pal. Fill 'em up.'

'White man speak heap shit,' Bob muttered. 'That not funny.'

'I'll go see to the horses,' Cass said, worried about his being stolen, but Guinevere was still there and the two men were swinging into the saddles of their own steeds. As they pulled away, Whispering Rick rode close and hissed, 'You int'rested in riding with

Colonel Anderson?'

Cass grinned, goofily. 'Maybe. Ain't got nuthin' else to do.'

'If I bump into him I'll pass the message on. You with that other guy?'

'Nah, I just bumped into him on the trail.'

'Get rid of him,' the whisper came.

Cass watched them ride off into the night. 'So long, fellas,' he called, mightily relieved they had gone. 'We ain't interested in you small fry. It's Anderson we're after.'

It occurred to him that Jim Clarke was too well-known in the Nations. Maybe he *should* go after them alone. It could be the only way he was going to get in close.

7

It was pitch dark in the stable in the early hours when Cass was woken by a tug on his boot. Indeed, he was being dragged from the heap of straw on which he had been sleeping, forcing him to leave his gunbelt and rifle where he had laid them. There was a whispering and rustling in the darkness. 'What's going on?' he hooted, still half-asleep and wondering if he might be dreaming. Then he, remembered. He had attached his lariat from the Palomino's neck to his ankle. Suddenly, in a glimmer of light across the doorway, he saw an Indian with a blanket over the mare's head leading her away, or trying to. 'Hold on there!'

But, as he shouted, the horse gave another tug away and it was just as well she did for a blunt instrument which otherwise might have smashed into his face, gave him a glancing blow to the side of his head as it thudded into the ground.

'Hell's teeth!' Cass cried and swung a desperate haymaker with his right fist in the general direction of his attacker, whoever it was. By luck his fist connected hard with solid flesh, possibly a jawbone, and he heard a gasp.

The young Texan followed up the attack, clambering to his feet and raining in blows with both fists at the shadowy shape by his side. By now his eyes had become slightly accustomed to the darkness, or else he could smell his assailant and sense his presence as his left fist thudded into his midriff.

But he could not see the arm raised again to strike and the skull-cracker hit him hard again to the top of his shoulder. Cass winced with pain and shock to his nerves but managed to hang on to the arm, wrestling for possession of the weapon. He kicked out his free boot, catching the man, he hoped, where it hurt.

But the mare had started stotting and pronking, all four hoofs leaving the ground as she pranced — a trick she might have learned as a rodeo show horse — and jerked Cass off his feet once more.

'What's going on?' Jim Clarke had come to his senses. He could hear the Palomino whinnying and saw the vague shape of the Indian trying to drag the mare from the stable. But he was not having it all his own way. 'Where the hell did I put my gun?' the sheriff muttered, searching frantically through the straw.

There was the faint glimmer of a scalping knife as the Indian slashed free the lariat restraining the horse, then leapt on her bare back, spinning her around. He hurled the knife at the sheriff, pinning him by his topcoat to a stall post. He gave a cry of victory and tried to turn the mare and head away into the night.

Cass's blood was up. He took a running jump and landed astraddle the mare's hind quarters. He had the lariat, still attached to one boot, and he looped it around the Ponca's throat, jerking it tight. 'I got him,' he yelled, as the Ponca flailed his arms.

At that moment the Palomino chose to go up on her hind legs, kicking out her front hoofs to shed her load. Cass slid from her back, taking the native with him, but managed to hold him and tightened the rawhide noose across his throat.

Suddenly the moon emerged from behind dark clouds, casting enough light for Clarke to see the shadowy shape of the Indian's accomplice, still grimacing from the kick in the groin, creeping forward behind Cass, his skull-cracker raised to administer the *coup de grâce*, or so he hoped.

Still pinned back to the post by the knife, Clarke had located his Thunderer where he had left it in his coat pocket. He raised the heavy gun high, arms outstretched, and carefully squeezed the trigger. Flame and death crashed out, the heavy slug smashing through one side of the Ponca's ribs and out the other side. His body, spilling blood, hurtled into a dung heap.

'Kill them,' Jim ordered, peering at the shadowy shapes on the ground. 'That's all hoss thieves deserve.'

Cass hesitated, but gritted his teeth and jerked the rawhide tight, cutting into his assailant's Adam's apple until he croaked no more.

There was the sound of voices and the light from a slopping lantern as Ponca Bob arrived, followed by the Indian woman and Ed Collins, a gun in his fist.

'Yeuk!' Cass's heart was beating fast as he rolled the dead Indian away and Clarke managed to free himself from the knife stuck in the post. 'I never trusted them two drunks from the start.'

'Your friends tried to kill us,' Jim explained to Bob. 'They shoulda done it 'fore they tried to steal the hoss. I hope this was nothing to do with you.'

'No friends me. Bad trouble.' Bob rolled one over with his foot then took a look at the other mouldering in the steamy dung. 'Them dead.'

'Yeah.' Clarke winced as he slipped off his topcoat and examined his bloody shirt. 'It's just a flesh wound. Lucky for me. His aim weren't too good.' He tore a strip from his shirt tail and bound it around the knife cut to his upper arm as Cass knotted it tight for him. 'You OK?'

'Not 'xactly.' Blood was trickling from Cass's head wound, dampening his hair. He pulled off his bandanna and pressed it tight. 'I'm gonna have some damn headache.' He picked up the weapon responsible, a smoothed stone bound by rawhide to a forked handle, and tossed it away. 'I guess we were both lucky. What a way to greet the morn.'

Ponca Bob looked worried. 'You go. Take bad men with you before my people come. No want trouble. Bad rubbish, but they got kin.'

Cass went out to retrieve the Palomino who had headed off down the street and came thudding back in response to his whistle. 'Steady, gal,' Cass soothed as she danced around, tossing her mane. 'I ain't gonna let no bad Injun git ya, no way.'

By the time he returned Clarke had already slung his baggage and the two corpses across the mule's strong back.

'Saddle up, *amigo*, we're going after them others.'

The sun's rays were flickering over the edge of the eastern horizon as they rode out, heading west. When they came to a handy ravine they paused to pitch the two bodies down into its undergrowth.

'That damn circus horse is gonna be a magnet in this Territory,' Clarke said, clambering back into his saddle. 'Come on, let's move. We got sixty miles to go to Cherokee.'

★ ★ ★

Before them stretched a great salt plain called Little Sahara where the going would be tough for both horse and man. They were glad to complete the twenty mile crossing, reach the other side and on to Cherokee. There the town chief broke the wall of silence, agreed the Raiders had been there, and with a few guttural words and signs pointed them on their way.

'Amazing how a plug of baccy loosens a man's tongue, ain't it?' Jim remarked. 'I allus carry a few gifts for the natives. It pays.'

They bore south-west, forded the Cimarron and eventually their horses' nostrils quivered eagerly as they scented the mighty Canadian River after another day's riding. The shades of night drew in, the evening air was chill and Cass, who like many cowboys had never learned to swim, looked doubtfully at the angry swirling waters in full flood melt of the snows that filled it from the slopes of the distant Rockies. But Clarke eagerly descended the bank, dragging his protesting mule on a trail rope, and without a second look spurred his mount in to breast the flow. Cass had no option but to follow. 'Come on, Guinevere,' he urged. 'You can do it.' Suddenly, as they reached centre point he was swept clean out of the saddle, going under in the numbing cold, coming up spitting water. The Palomino drifted towards him and he grabbed a stirrup as she made valiantly for the far bank.

'Hell's bells!' Cass's teeth chattered as he finally made the shore. 'I'm freezin'.'

'Yeah, I saw you was having fun.' Jim grinned, tipping the water out of his boots, but otherwise reasonably dry.

'You better strip off and dry your clothes. We'll build a fire beneath them rocks. Good place to stay the night.'

The Wichita sheriff was a man who liked a tad of comfort when he lived rough, coming prepared with padded soogans for sleeping in and a big water-proof groundsheet which he would rig up like a tent when it poured. He kept his spare clothes, shirt, socks, underwear dry, rolled up in his rubberized riding cape, and tossed a blanket at Cass as he shivered naked. Clarke soon found kindling and had a blaze going in a trice. He rigged up a trellis of greenwood sticks and laid the Texan's wet jeans, shirt, socks and long johns across.

'You take it easy, young'un,' he grinned, picking up his shotgun. 'I'll go see about catching our supper.'

There was a burst of gunfire from all three barrels, and not long before the sheriff returned bearing a brace of prairie grouse. 'Here, git these plucked and gutted.' He tossed them at Cass. 'I ain't here to wet nurse ya.'

Cass felt a tad sissyish sat there on a rock wrapped in the rough blanket, but at least his shivers had stopped and he guessed it was better than, as his mother would say, catching his death of cold. The fire was blazing high so he went to work with a will, sticking his fist up the birds' backsides to rip out their

116

guts, tossing those onto the flames to avoid attracting bears and covering himself with feathers as he plucked the birds. Soon they had them roasting with an appetizing scent in the fire's glow.

The sheriff picked one up on its greenwood spit and took a bite, spitting out skin and bones. 'Yep, mighty tasty. Help yaself.'

Cass fished out his grouse and tore off a wing. 'You sure don't need much cash when you live in the wild.'

'So huccome you're broke? Ain't Brady been paying you your wages?'

'No, it ain't that. I had near on sixty bucks saved. But I'm in the same boat as everybody else: it was in the Eureka bank. Now its in the pockets of them lousy crooks.'

Darkness had closed in and they listened to the shrill sounds of critters up in the woods behind them, the eternal battle of the hunters and the hunted. 'I been thinking maybe I should go ahead, get in with this bunch.'

'Just where the hell do you think you're gonna go? You better give up on that idea until we've some idea where they are.' Clarke gazed at the glow of the fire as he aired his socks. 'Was that true about your daddy killed at Antietam? You sounded pretty convincing and bitter about Old Glory.'

'They say the dead was piled up in droves so he weren't the only one. Sure, I seen the South in ruins. Folks down my way suffered pretty bad. But, no, I guess the war's over now. We gotta put it behind us, be one nation.'

Cass started to get back into his somewhat scorched garments, buckling the belt of his jeans and pulling on his buckskin jacket over his shirt. 'No, I didn't mean that about the flag. I was just acting. You figure I could convince Anderson I wanna fight on?'

'I ain't so sure about that. It would be mighty risky.'

'Waal, we gotta take risks.' Cass knelt to fish the coffee pot from the embers. 'Sure glad I didn't lose my hat. Lucky I had the cord round my chin when I took a dive. Still, I guess it all washed out a few bugs.' The coffee pot singed his fingers and keeled over as he dropped it. 'Shit!'

'Look what you're doing, boy,' Clarke admonished, passing his tin mug across.

'Ain't lost much.'

Jim wrapped himself in his soogans, leaning back against his saddle. 'I went off banks a long time ago. Don't trust 'em. I keep what bit I got in gold coin in a pot hidden in the yard. Anything happens to me my missus knows where it is. Not that it's much. That's why I'm on this fool expedition.'

'Brady figures you're making a fortune from fining the whores in Wichita and from protection money. Sounded real jealous, said you were raking in two thousand a month.'

'He did, did he? Waal, you can tell him most of that went into the town council's coffers, plus I had to pay my deputies, so there weren't a lot left. The wife's on to me to retire, hang up my guns, buy a patch of land. But I cain't afford to unless we come up trumps with a bit of reward cash.'

Jim fell silent, lighting his corncob pipe and taking a sup of the black coffee Cass handed him. He stared at the rippling sheen of the black river as, like a great serpent, it coiled around a bend. 'It ain't much fun gitting old.'

* * *

'You what?' Colonel Anderson roared. 'You were face to face with that Wichita sheriff and you let him off the hook? That's the killer who put poor Spotty Jed in his grave. That boy was barely sixteen, a true southern patriot if ever I seen one.'

'The big man?' Josiah Baines asked. 'Outside Wells Fargo?'

'Yes, I've heard about the brave Sheriff Clarke and his shotgun.'

'That's him,' Jawbone whined. 'He had us covered. Would *you* face a shotgun at close quarters?'

'True,' Whispering Rick put in. 'And he had some sidekick we weren't sure about.'

'So, why didn't you wait for 'em? Ambush 'em on the trail?'

'Holy Jazus, Colonel,' Jawbone protested. 'We weren't sceered. We would've but you tol' us yourself you didn't want no unnecessary killing.'

'What you think a damn sheriff is, you numbskull? He's necessary. I want Clarke dead. That's an order.'

'The other one didn't sound like he was siding him. Said he had just met him on the trail. In fact, Colonel, he sounded like a boy after your own heart. A regular Southern Reb. Lost his daddy at Antietam.'

'A likely story. Are you gullible, or what, Mr Hudson? Or could you be plain stupid?'

'Aw, no need to be like that, J.G. I just thought he'd make a good replacement for Jed.'

'You thought! Leave the thinking to me. And don't call me J.G. Mr Baines is

121

by way of being a personal comrade. To you I'm Colonel, or sir.'

'Yes, suh, Colonel, suh!' Jawbone saluted, sarcastically, and sauntered out of the echoing alabaster cave they had made their hideout.

One day alabaster from these pure white walls would be used to make fine statuary but until now the caves were known only to the Indians and a few backwoodsmen, one of whom had shown them to Anderson who had then shot the man to preserve the secret.

'Jawbone would have been put up before a firing squad in the war for desertion, insolence and disobeying orders. I told him not to go back to Ponca City.'

'Where the hell else we gonna get a jug of whuskey or a dame?' Whispering Rick growled and went to join his pal outside.

'Next time they'll get a damn good flogging.'

'Aw, why give 'em so much cash? It goes to their heads,' Baines told the colonel, looking around at young Mace Underwood and the older man, Skeeter Hardy, who muttered, 'Them two need disciplining.'

They had made reasonably comfortable beds for themselves of spruce branches' wiry needle foliage covered with blankets on which they sprawled. But they were impatient. Randy Sims posed the question on all their minds. 'So, what do we do now? We can't lie low here for ever. Somebody's going to see our fire smoke.'

'We're not finished yet,' Anderson informed them. 'We're going to make one more strike.'

'So, what's that?'

'A paymaster's wagon coming from Fort Supply in the north down to Fort Reno carrying not only guns and ammunition which we can sell to the Apaches, but soldiers' wages as well.'

'What?' the disgruntled Randy screeched. 'You're gonna make war on the whole of the US Army now? Are you totally mad? They'll hunt us down. Not me, bud. I want out. I'm gettin' the hell back outa this wilderness. I'm a city lover.'

Josiah Baines gave his creepy grin and connected with Anderson's glance as if to agree a secret message. 'You ain't going nowhere,' he whispered, sibilantly. 'What, and start blabbing all you know about us and the whereabouts of this cave to the first sheriff you meet?'

'Mr Sims will come with us,' Anderson said. 'When we've taken the paymaster's wagon we'll go south. I've another hideout down there among the Wichita mountains and lakes. Then we will return to Texas. You, Mr Sims, can then go where the hell you like.'

8

Before the Civil War sixty million buffalo had roamed the central plains. Now there were less than six million and most of those were on the prairies to the north. White-men's greed and political cynicism had presided over the widescale slaughter that had deprived the nomadic tribes of their sustenance. A few proud warriors, Sioux to the north and Apache on the southern borders, fought on, but most had been forced to accept defeat, were herded on to reservations and lived on handouts, attempting to adapt to a sedentary life.

With a sweep of his hand Jim Clarke indicated the vast stretch of lush grass they had crossed. 'What a waste of damned fine ranchland. It's made little use of now by the tribes. No wonder so many white settlers are straining at the leash to get in. I'd like to put down roots here myself.'

Of course, there were still a few renegades about, young bucks with an urge to roam and steal horses, but the army's howitzers had knocked the fighting spirit out of the majority.

As they jogged across the plain under dark louring clouds Cass suddenly got a prickling feeling in the hairs at the back of his neck. He peered at a range of hills not far off to the west. 'How about we take a look over there,' he called.

'Aw, no,' Jim shouted back. 'I figure they've gone south-west.'

A mile away Jawbone Hudson rested the barrel of his Long Tom on a rock and squinted through a 'scope fitted to its top — at a cost of $200. 'It's that lowdown sheriff,' he drawled. 'Didn't the colonel say we gotta kill him?'

'Bit of a risky long shot from here.' Whispering Rick was crouched down with him in their hidey-hole in the rocks keeping watch. 'Better let 'em go.'

Jawbone thumbed down the hammer of the powerful Sharps single shot rifle, chambered for .45-.70 cartridges much favoured by buff hunters, and lined up the sights on the head of Clacy who had ridden up alongside his friend. 'I bet I could blast the daylights outa that cocky damn cowboy. I figure J.G. was right. He's been foolin' us.'

Rick put a restraining hand on his arm. 'Let's follow. We got more chance if we get close up . . . of killin' 'em both.'

★   ★   ★

The prairie funnelled into the Washita Valley which was more forested, had game in abundance, but with little sign of human habitation. Before darkness the two lawmen, now bounty hunters, made camp on the bank of the meandering stream. Cass cast a line and maggot-baited hook over to a pool where flies hovered tempting fish to snatch at them. Before long he had two fine rainbow trout frizzling over the ashes for supper.

Jim tossed his fish bones into the fire's embers. 'You look a lot better for being away from the rotgut whiskey and them loose wimmin. A spell in the wide open spaces'll do us both good.'

'True. I needed a break,' Cass said. 'I been having second thoughts about going back.'

'Why? Marshal Brady getting on your nerves?'

'Not just that. To tell the truth it's woman trouble. I been seeing one who's married with kids and it's getting a trifle heavy. Her husband's on the warpath.'

'Anybody I know?'

'Er . . . not really.'

'You've only yourself to blame.' Clarke and his wife were stalwart Wichita Baptists. He gave him a severe look. 'I don't approve of behaviour like that. Haven't you any moral scruples? What makes you want to go with a married woman?'

'Waal, they're cheaper for a start. No upkeep required. No hankering for all them baubles, bangles and beads unmarried gals go on about. An' they're easier. They like the attention and are generally willing.'

'That disgusts me. Only trollops behave like that. I've been married twenty-five years and I trust my wife implicitly. She believes in her marriage vows. Why don't you settle down with a decent gal?'

Cass got up and broke dead pine to feed the fire. 'I ain't got the time for romancing, Jim. All that sitting around on the porch holding hands and when you try to git friendly all you get is a squawk. Hell, you know what us cowboys say. Love 'em, lay 'em and leave 'em. We don't like being tied down.'

'Sounds to me more like ye'll be laid down in your grave if that husband catches up.'

'Yeah,' Cass grinned. 'That's why I'm rolling on.'

Suddenly a voice rang out from the darkness of the woods. 'Hi, there, the camp. Can we come in?'

It was a precaution taken by anyone on the range, but Clarke got to his feet, uneasily, glancing at Cass and reaching for the Thunderer in its holster, easing the hammer back to half-cock. 'Who's there?' he shouted.

'Howdy, fellers.' Two horsemen showed themselves on the edge of the fire's flickering circle.

'Looks like we're all headed in the same direction, don't it?' Jawbone drawled.

'Step down,' Jim growled at him and his companion. 'Guess we can spare you varmints a mug of coffee. Then you better keep on going.'

'That ain't hospitable.' Whispering Rick stepped down but stood well away, barely out of the shadow of the trees and his hands hovered over the yellowed ivory grips of his twin .44s.

'Ain't you got any grub?' Jawbone asked.

'Ye're too late fer supper. We just ate it.' The sheriff pointed at the hook and line. 'There's plenty of fish in the river. Go try your luck. Then go cook it five miles away from here. I'm choosy about the company I keep.'

'What you mean by that?' Jawbone whined, one hand snaking across towards the Rigson-Ansley pistol on his belt. 'That don't sound like you wants us as friends.'

Cass carefully tipped coffee into their own two mugs and placed them on a fallen tree trunk. 'So you boys are after the Anderson gang, too?'

'You could say so,' Rick whispered, still on the edge of the circle, unwilling to step in close.

'Here y'are. Best Jalapa beans.' Jim picked up one of the mugs and passed it to Jawbone. 'Be grateful for God's mercies.'

'Yuh?' The gangling Jawbone reached for the mug but as he did so Clarke hurled the steaming contents in his face. Jawbone howled and clutched at his eyes. 'Aagh!'

Jim swiftly relieved him of his gun

from his belt with one hand and with his right pulled out his gun, aiming, without warning, at Rick.

Nervous as a cat, Cass backed away, going for his Five Shot, but his fish-greasy hands slipped on the smooth walnut grip. 'Hot damn!' he yelled, for Rick was blazing away with both his .44s out of the darkness. Cass dived for the cover of the log as bullets buzzed about him like bees.

Jim grabbed Jawbone's scruff and pulled him before him as a shield. He held his right arm out erect and blasted four more from the powerful .41 at the gunfire from the wood's shadow.

Cass had finally got hold of his Never Miss and thrust his arm over the log, firing, too.

Their assailant's dark shape appeared to throw up his hands and crash over into the undergrowth. There was an ominous silence.

'Is he dead?' Jim called. 'Or playing possum?'

Cass circled back into the wood and

cautiously poked the body with his boot. 'He's dead, all right.'

'Who got him?'

'I think we both did.'

Jawbone was cursing, blindly trying to stumble about. Clarke jerked him back, tripped him and booted him in the gut. 'Like to kill us, would ya? Who are you? Where's Anderson? Are there any more of your pals out there?' He peered apprehensively out into the dark woods as Jawbone grovelled on the sod.

'We're bounty hunters,' Jawbone pleaded, his fingers touching his red-scorched face. 'Same as you. There ain't nobody else.'

'There better not be or they'll know what they get.' Clarke smashed his gun into Hudson's lantern jaw. 'Start talking. The truth this time. Or you want the same treatment?'

'No, please.' Jawbone spat out blood and teeth. 'I don't know nuthin'.'

'You asked for it.' Clarke picked up the coffee pot with its rag and tipped it over Jawbone's legs. 'You're with

Anderson, aincha? Where is he. You want some more?'

'No,' Jawbone begged. 'He's at his hideout down in the Wichita Mountains.'

'Whereabouts? That's a big domain.'

'I don't know.' Then Jawbone screamed as the sheriff tipped scalding coffee on to his genital area. 'Ketch Lake! I'm telling you the truth. He got a cabin there.'

'You better be. I don't wanna waste any more best Jalapa. Who killed the Caldwell storekeeper?'

'It wasn't me. It was Josiah Baines. He's crazy.'

'What's your name?'

'Hudson. Jim Hudson.'

'And who's he?'

'Whispering Rick. That's all I know.' Jawbone quivered and sobbed as the sheriff pressed the Magnum to his temple. 'Please don't — '

'Rest in peace.' Clarke grimly squeezed the trigger and blew Jawbone's head into a mess of blood and bones, the

brain pan spilling a grey ooze like por-
ridge. 'May your sins be absolved.'

Cassius Clacy stared at him in
shocked silence. It was a side of Clarke
he had never imagined. 'Did you have
to do that?'

'Why? Did you want to take 'em back
to Wichita?' The sheriff turned his
watery eyes on him. 'What mercy did
they show that lady in Eldorado? The
shopkeeper and his wife in Caldwell?'

As the gunsmoke drifted he added, 'I
only take prisoners if they got a decent
price on their heads. These two no
accounts ain't. Gimme a hand.'

He examined Rick's twin S&Ws.
'Nice guns. Want them? I'll have his
cartridges. They cost twenty-five cents
apiece these days. Terrible price.' He
picked up Hudson's Rigsdon-Ansley.
'Southern-made crap.' He tossed it into
the bushes. 'Some Indian will be glad to
give a few bucks for their mounts. Well,
goodness me! Ain't these boys in the
money?' He pulled rumpled greenbacks
from their pockets and counted up.

'More'n one thousand six hundred dollars 'tween 'em. I'll return this to Wells Fargo. You want anything? Or are you too finicky?'

'I sure got a big hole in my boot.' Cass pulled off Rick's tooled black leather ones. 'Yeah, just my size.' In the end he took his nearly brand new hat, his black embroidered shirt and his .44s.

'Git hold of his ankles.' The sheriff hoisted the corpse and they carried it to the river, tossing it in. They did the same with Jawbone. 'Don't wanna attract no bears in the night. Now we can sleep peaceful. Where's that coffee pot?'

Cass watched the black humps of corpses slowly float away, taken by the moonlit sheen of the current towards the river's bend. 'So long, boys.' He went back to the fire. 'I'll boil up a fresh pot.'

Coffee had never tasted so bitter. 'I guess it was them,' he whispered, 'or us.'

*   *   *

He didn't sleep easy and rose in the murky dawn hearing a sound. But it was only a buck leading his harem of does and young out of the trees and down the slope, his rack of antlers probing the mist. They nibbled at grass through the hoar frost, daintily flowing past, steam rising from their hides, white under-tails bobbing as they disappeared into the trees.

Cass could easily have brought one down. But it would be too big and bulky and a bother to carry, so he let them go. And, somehow, it didn't seem right to shatter such an idyllic scene.

The two new bounty hunters spoke little as they headed on their way south-west, Clarke pondering the information he had gleaned, Cass wondering what the hell he had gotten into. As they pressed on through the lush Washita valley they came across the occasional Indian settlement. Not tee-pees but rundown cabins, runty ponies, yapping dogs and litter. It was not long since the ill-famed attack by Custer and his 7th Cavalry on Black Kettle's peaceful village. The Cheyenne were sleeping they thought, under the protection of the Stars and Stripes flag when a hundred men, women and children were slaughtered, and 900 ponies killed. Now a kind of apathy reigned. They had had the stuffing knocked out of them, sure enough.

Jim Clarke had no difficulty disposing of the two horses, even scribbling out a rough bill of sale. He put his finger to his lips to indicate the obvious and rode on. There was so far no sign of the other men they sought. Towards sundown they cantered their horses into an area of red rock canyons.

'Looks like we'd better go along here.' The sheriff led the way along a narrow Indian trail on the side of a precipitous cliff below which the river tumbled on its course. Suddenly Guinevere stopped in her tracks, her ears pricked forward, her whole body trembling, sweat breaking out on her flanks. There was a rustle in the undergrowth of ponderosas on a ledge above them and a low growl. The enemy a horse feared most.

'Watch out!' Cass shouted, pulling his heavy Creedmore from the boot, bringing it upwards as the yellow-skinned big cat leapt out and on to the mule's back. Cass fired and pack mule and scrabbling, snarling mountain lion went tumbling head over heels down the shale. As suddenly the mule hit the fork of a sturdy pine that blocked their descent. Cass pumped in another round. The cougar leapt in agony and lay still. 'I think I got him,' he said. 'Poor ol' Lop Ears. I'll go see if I can get him back up.'

The mule was upturned, kicking his hoofs and braying indignantly, his pack firmly stuck in the pine's fork. 'Easy, boy,' Cass said. 'I'm gonna cut you free.'

Jim had slithered down to join him. 'Good Lord! Look at the teeth on that!'

The big cat was spread out, his face a howl from the bloody heart shot. 'He's a hell of a size. If you hadn't been quick on the trigger ol' Lop Ears would have been in a mess. Think we can get him back up?'

It was difficult but soon the mule was righted and back on the track. They put a rope on the cougar and on the pack and hauled them up. Then they slung the extra load of the cat across Lop Ears' shoulders. 'Forward,' Jim cried. 'You got y'self quite a trophy, boy.'

9

It was getting late in the day when they followed a pass through the Wichita mountains and reached the shore of Kiowa Lake, or so Clarke reckoned from his rough map for it was new territory to him. Suddenly they heard the vibrant strains of a violin drifting through a stand of evergreens, magical in such a setting.

'Where on earth's that coming from?' Jim wondered. 'Am I hearing things?'

The music grew louder, more frenetic, as they followed the shoreline and saw, set back among the pines, about six acres of fenced fields. In its midst was a ramshackle cabin with a high-pitched roof slated with bark, and a stone-built chimney from which smoke trickled. To Cass it looked like something out of a fairy-tale.

The music had grown louder, more

soulful and plangent and drew them in through rough gateposts up a path towards the house. 'You stay right where y'are,' a shrill voice struck out. 'You varmints ain't wanted here.'

When they reined in a lanky girl appeared out of the dusk, vaulted the pole fence with long bare legs and waved an ancient musket at them. 'Turn them hosses round and clear off. You'll keep on going if you know what's good for you.'

'Hang on, missy, we don't mean you no harm.' Cass grinned at her. 'We was just wondering where the concert's coming from.'

'That's my daddy practisin' and he don't like to be disturbed.' The girl had a prow of a nose jutting out beneath ash-blonde hair that was pulled up into a pony-tail that dangled from the top of her head. Her homespun dress was skimpy to the extreme, as if it had been sawn off above the knees, and her bare legs terminated in Indian moccasins. 'What's the matter, you deaf? I tol' ya, we don't take kindly to intruders with guns, so you better be off 'fore I blow y'all to smithereens.'

Jim frowned down on her. 'Now wait a minute. I'm a lawman, a sheriff, here on legitimate business. We ain't aiming to hurt you or your folks. So don't you go gittin' an itchy finger on that trigger, gal. You go tell your pa we'd be glad to barter for a bite to eat 'fore we go on our way.'

'Barter?' she scoffed. 'What with?'

Jim pointed back at the cougar spawled across the mule's back. 'That, for starters, would make y'all a nice fur rug.'

'Ah! Poor thing.' She stepped close to stroke the side of the big cat. 'What you done to the poor critter?'

'You'd have shot him, too,' Cass put in, 'if he was trying to eat your mule.'

The young woman stared at him, defiantly, as if trying to take all this in. 'You two stay here. I'll go see Pa.' She backed away, then raced off on her long legs to the cabin. The door opened and closed and the music ceased. The door reopened and a stumpy, middle-aged man came out, what looked like a gnarled walking stick in his hand. He limped towards them. 'Howdy-doo,' he called, his face as wrinkled as a walnut beneath his shock of white hair. 'What is it you want here?'

'We're lawmen, mister.' Cass fished out his tin star to show him. 'I'm Cassius Clacy, Deputy Sheriff of Eureka. This here's Mr Jim Clarke, Sheriff of Wichita. We ain't gonna hurt you none.'

The man studied their faces. 'I was in the middle of Dvorak's *Humoresque*. I am, perhaps, still there. John Wesley Cox is the name. Why don't you join us for supper?'

'That's mighty friendly.' Clarke swung down from the saddle. 'Would this be Kiowa Lake? We're looking for Ketch Lake.'

'That's a good way away. There's a network of lakes throughout these mountains. If you want to, leave your horses in the barn.'

'Yeah, well, we won't unpack. We was planning to bed down along on the shore.'

'No,' John Wesley insisted. 'You can sleep in there. You have honest faces. Show them the stalls, Daughter. We've plenty of splitcorn to feed their mounts.'

'Thought maybe you might like this cougar that attacked us up back on the trail. I'll skin him for ya in the mornin' if ya want. Meanwhile I'll hoist him up on a branch outa reach of the bears.'

'Yes, by all means. He might make a cover for the bed. Come on inside when you're washed up.'

The girl eyed Cass suspiciously as she dug a scoop into a bin for corn and fed the mounts as he unsaddled and removed the mule's pack. 'My daddy's too trusting, but you seem all right,' she scowled.

'We got two more for supper, Elisabeth,' Mr Cox called, as he took them inside.

The place was remarkably tidy, as they say, neat as a new pin. There were curtains at the windows, a fire burning merrily in the hearth, and a jam-jar of wild-flowers on the table.

'You can put the musket away now, Audrey,' John Wesley said, as a little woman appeared from the kitchen, her hair and long dress neat and tidy, too. 'This here's my sister . . . and my wife.'

The two bounty-hunters' heads swivelled expecting another lady to appear, but none arrived. Cass could barely suppress a grin as he drawled, 'Howdy, ma'am. Mighty kind of ya to have us.'

When she had returned to the kitchen and was clattering about, talking to Audrey or, it sounded more like, ordering her around, Jim Clarke said, 'Could I just get this clear, suh? That lady's your sister and your wife?'

'Yes. Elisabeth is my sister and she carries out a wife's duties, too, you know, cooking, washing, milking and those kinda things.'

'And Audrey is your daughter?'

'To be accurate, Elisabeth's daughter. It was long ago, before the war, '57, I think. We hadn't been here long. Of course, it was a much better place in those days, proper tribal law. Elisabeth suddenly found that she was with child. Most mysterious. I truly believe it must have been a virgin birth. The Lord had visited her in the night. So, what could I do but agree to act as husband and father?'

'What else?' Cass commented. 'The Lord acts in mysterious ways, don't he?'

Audrey, followed by a scruffy lurcher with an amputated rear left leg, had come from the kitchen and was stood listening.

'Put another log on the fire, girl. Don't just stand there.' John Wesley lowered his voice with a grimace. 'She's a little slow in the head. Odd, you might say.'

'Mm.' Cass watched the young woman bend over the fire. Her dress was as short as an Indian woman's and he couldn't help but be transfixed by her shapely rump, and expanse of bare white thigh and calves. 'Mighty fine,' he murmured. 'Think of something else!'

The black-eye beans, the greens on platters, and crisply browned fish pie were mighty fine, too. Seemed like the family ate a lot of fish because Audrey hated her pa killing animals, all that blood. It made her cry. Yeah, she was very odd, Cass thought, because most folk he knew would love to get their chops around a three-inch-thick juicy steak. But he couldn't take his eyes off the girl. For some reason she fascinated him.

'Do you take cream in your coffee, mister?' she asked, as she stood to clear the wooden bowls.

'Wow, you durn tootin', honey. Now you really got my mouth watering,' Cass yelled, laughing at her look of surprise.

'We don't go in for fancy desserts, 'cept when there's fruits in season,' John Wesley said. 'But we got a nice goat's cheese and crackers if you gents would like to partake.'

'No chance, I suppose,' Clarke prompted, 'of a drop of the hard stuff?'

'Oh no, we don't believe in that. The devil's handiwork.'

'Too true,' Clarke sighed, stirring his coffee, loosening his belt. 'This has been most enjoyable. I take it you're from England, Mr Cox.'

'Yes, Elisabeth and I hail from the county of Dorset. We took ship from Portsmouth. A dreadful voyage. Icebergs. Gales. Two months of misery. Stayed for a while in New York. Awful place. A babble of tongues. So we headed West and kept going. We wanted to get as far away as we could from mankind's follies and wars. At first it seemed that we had found our goal here. We had a licence to trade. The tribes were self-governing and welcomed us. But then war broke out between the states and everything went haywire. We lost most of what we had to what the Confederate Cherokee soldiers termed foraging. I'd call it downright theft.'

'But we survived,' Elisabeth put in, her eyes shining fervently. 'The Lord's name be praised.'

Clarke got up and went to warm his backside before the fire. 'But don't the Union soldiers bother you?'

'No, they let us be,' John Wesley said. 'Of course, I know we have no legal entitlement to these acres. But I hear there's change in the air and if we hang on maybe we will get ownership of our own farm.'

'It'll be some while yet,' Clarke said. 'Ain't you had no trouble from the tribes?'

Audrey had been listening. 'Healing Woman says they're sceered of Pa's violin music. They think it comes from the Other World.'

'Who's she?'

'A friend of Audrey's,' Cox snapped. 'For sure, the girl's turning into a veritable Indian herself. We're at our wits' end what to do with her.'

'Healing Woman knows a lot of things,' Audrey responded. 'She teaches me about all the plants and the animals. She hears voices in the wind.'

'You'd better help your mother tidy up. These gentlemen might like to smoke before they retire.'

When the women had gone into the kitchen Cass remarked, 'Your daughter don't have much resemblance to you two. I mean she's so pale and slim and blonde-haired . . . '

'Yes, thereby lies a tale,' John Wesley mused, puffing at his clay pipe. 'It lies heavy on my conscience. Could I have your assurance, if I should tell you, that you will not repeat this?'

'Sure,' Clarke said. 'What's bothering you?'

'Well, it so happens, before the Big War there was another Englishman settled here. The Indians had little animosity to us in those days. It was a good life. I am of yeoman stock and reasonably well-schooled. This young fellow, Henry FitzAlan, was a different

151

breed, what we call a remittance man, pretty young wife and allowance from his family. So happened she became pregnant at the same time as Elisabeth. Henry and I had become good friends and we often visited each other. The Lord smiled on us and both women produced healthy offspring. Henry's wife had a daughter. And Elisabeth a son.

'Yeah, interesting,' Clarke mused. 'I'm gittin' an inkling of where this is going.'

'Indeed,' John Wesley went on. 'One night Henry revealed to me that his brother was a Lord FitzAlan, who owned vast estates in the county of Yorkshire, with rich coal fields beneath them. Also London properties. His brother had, however, died in a hunting accident and he had come into the title and had to return to England. Henry told me that his own health was not too good. He suffered from some incurable disease he would not be specific about.

'He needed a male heir to inherit if

anything should happen to him.'

'Ah, I getcha,' Cass exclaimed. 'A cradle swap.'

'Exactly. Henry offered me a large sum in gold there and then if he could take our boy back with him and he would leave his baby girl here with me. What can I say? Who would not be tempted by such an offer? I fear to say I succumbed. The transaction went through. A bit of bribery produced false birth certificates, all hush hush. That was the last we saw of our son. To my eternal regret we were left with this silly creature . . . this girl. Oh, she means no harm, but . . . '

His 'wife' and 'daughter' had gone out to lock up the animals and had returned with buckets of water from the well, hauling them into the back kitchen.

'I fear I have bored you,' John Wesley said. 'I think I will practise my violin a little more before I turn in.'

'Not at all,' Clarke drawled. 'It ain't none of our business but it's a mighty interesting story.'

'Sure is,' Cass agreed. 'Very strange, indeed.'

* * *

The family's four milch cows, two goats and numerous chickens had been herded into the barn for safety over-night and at first glimmer of dawn young Audrey opened up. What with all the animals the barn had become pretty smelly so Cass got up to help her herd the cows and goats back to the pasture.

'Summer's on its way,' he said, as the sun's rays flickered up over the horizon. 'I guess gitting up for this ain't much fun in the winter.'

'I don't mind,' she sang out. 'I like the snow. It's real pretty. Out here on my own I can practise my Indian prayin' like Healing Woman has taught me.' She raised her hands in the air turning in a circle chanting, '*To ma tus to nuk ka*!' Then she hawked and spat into the centre of the circle, stepping out. 'You see them hills over there? That's the holy city of the Wichitas. Healing Woman's promised to take me up there when they have a real ceremony one day.'

As she turned she bumped into Cass and he caught hold of her waist. 'You know somethang,' he said. 'You're real pretty, too.'

'Me?' She snorted with merriment as if the idea was absurd and went to push past him. 'I ain't pretty.'

'Yes, y'are.' He pulled her into the wood and pressed her back against a big pine tree. 'You're beautiful.'

'What? Git orf me.' She struggled, gawkily, turning her head back and forth to escape his lips as he tried to kiss her. 'What you doing?'

'Doncha like kissing?' He had hold of both of her hands and held her tight. 'It's real fun.'

'No, it ain't.' She struggled against him. 'I know what kissing does. Don't think I'm silly. You git babies from kissing.'

'You need to do more than that.' He grinned at her naivety. 'Come on, give it a try.'

'No.' She screwed up her eyes and gripped her lips firmly together. 'You don't stop I'm gonna scream for my pa. He'll be real mad.'

Audrey thrust him away. 'I know what you're up to. Don't think I don't. I ain't stupid.' She jumped out on to the path, stared back at him for moments, then raced away.

'Oh, Gawd!' Cass watched her go. 'Now she'll go squawking to her ma.'

But when he got back to the barn she was there mucking out. 'I'll help you,' he said, grabbing a shovel and scraping up the gooey mess to tip into a barrow. He didn't say any more until they were done. They took a rest, standing together by the dungheap. 'Audrey,' he said. 'I didn't mean to frighten ya. It's just that you do something to me. I've never felt like this before. I just want you.'

She stood and stared at him, severely,

wiping a strand of hair from her eyes. 'But you're riding on. I'll never see you again.'

'Come on, Cass. Get your damn horse saddled up.' Clarke came from the barn and shouted at him. 'Leave that gal alone. I'm ready to go.'

'OK. I'm coming.' Briskly he attended to Guinevere, swung into the saddle. As they moved out he grinned at her. 'I'll be back,' he yelled.

'Don't believe a word this cowboy says, sweetheart,' Clarke shouted at her. 'He's got a married woman waiting for him back in Eureka.' Jim suddenly slashed his wrist-quirt across Guinevere's hind quarters. 'Geeit! Let's go!' The Palomino sprang away, bucking and zig-zagging, surprising Cass.

He managed to stay in the saddle and pull in the feisty mare when he reached the trail. He spun her around and up on her back legs, sweeping off his new Stetson to wave and give a rebel yell. 'So long!' he cried. Audrey was standing by her barrow, her three-legged dog by her side, her shovel in her hands, watching forlornly. But she returned his wave, which gave him heart, and, giving Guinevere her head, he put her to a gallop, charging away along the shore of the lake.

After a mile or so he slowed to let the sheriff and his mule catch up. 'Blabbing like that about me weren't friendly, Jim,' he accused.

'I'm protecting that innocent child. What you gonna do, cowboy, waltz her into the woods, then forget her like you say you do?'

'She ain't a child. She's the same age as me, and as tall, and purty strong, too. She can make her own decisions. You told me to find a decent gal and settle down. Well, I think I've found one. I like her. I really do.'

'Yeah, tell that to the squirrels,' Clarke growled. 'Stick to saloon whores and married sluts, Cass. They're more your style.'

10

Colonel John G. Anderson hadn't earned much in the way of battle honours during the war, nor even achieved the notoriety of his scallywag brother, Bloody Bill, one of Quantrill's Raiders, who led the massacre at Lawrence, Kansas, of 150 civilians. Indeed, as a slave holder he was in a reserved occupation and could have stayed at home picking cotton. Instead he had led his fifty black boys off to war, crossed the Mississippi, and was put in charge of building railroads to transport men and supplies to the front.

''Massa', old Mose said to me. 'Why don't you give us rifles not shovels, then we can fight for the folks we know. We don't want no strangers comin' down South tellin' us what to do'. You remember that, don't you, Josiah?'

'Sure do, J.G.,' Baines drawled, as he

bit into a plug of tobacco and chawed.

'You see, Mr Sims, things weren't like you folks up North like to imagine it was. And what did you get by freein' the slaves? Just a helluva lot of trouble, that's what. I bumped into old Mose one day after they set him loose. 'Massa', he said, 'I wish we could go back to the way things used to be'.'

'Sure,' Randy commented, with a distinct lack of enthusiasm. 'You don't say? I thought you said you commanded Confederate cavalry at Missionary Ridge and Lookout Mountain and saw some of the worst fighting of the war.'

His words echoed around the big, white-walled cave where three of his four companions had robed themselves in rebel uniform once more.

'That was later,' Josiah Baines snarled. 'They drafted us up there when thangs started to go wrong. You tryin' to be funny?'

'No,' Randy protested. 'But all that fightin' didn't seem to do you much good in the long run, did it? Y'all got squarely whupped.'

Baines pounced on him, gripping the New Yorker by the throat like a terrier with a rat. 'I'm gonna — '

'Sergeant!' Anderson snapped out. 'That's enough.'

Baines had his Bowie out and at Sims's throat, but froze. 'I'll stick this fat hog and slit him from gut to gizzard the next time — '

'Put that knife away. We need every man we've got, even Mr Sims. We've waited long enough. Those other two have deserted the cause.'

'I don't blame 'em.' Randy was coughing, holding his throat. 'You're all madmen.'

Anderson picked up a Marlin carbine with an English walnut stock, its tarn engraved with inlays in gold and silver of galloping horses, one of his most prized possessions. 'We have checked our weapons, our mounts are in fine fettle. We will proceed without Jawbone and Rick. My information is the paymaster's wagon should be passing this way at about noon on this very day. We will ambush it along at the ridge. We can do it, boys.'

'If we can't,' Randy moaned, picking up his own carbine, 'we ain't gonna be seeing no tomorrow.'

'We have no time for defeatist talk. We will be striking a blow at our mortal enemy, the Union Army.'

'Big deal,' Randy muttered, as he ambled off after them out of the cave and into the sunlight. He blinked up at it as if these might be his last few moments on earth.

★   ★   ★

The raid was, as Randy had forecast, a disaster. The waiting was bad enough cramped down in the grass and rocks, hour after hour as high noon passed and the sun crept on into the afternoon. They were about to give up when suddenly the wagon was sighted trundling along across the prairie, a shotgun guard sitting up beside the driver. Six troopers on army plugs were on the flanks.

'Hold your fire, men,' Colonel Anderson commanded. He had decided to give them an opening fusillade from the hillside to dismount as many as possible. 'Right, Skeeter . . . now!'

The 9th Louisiana Cavalry had been raised in '62 and Skeeter had been one of their crack sharpshooters. His grooved and seemingly weather-eroded face had the melancholy look of a man accustomed to sudden death. He rested the barrel of his Winchester on a rock and squinted along the sights. Lovingly he squeezed the trigger. Within a trice the head of the shotgun guard exploded in a shower of blood.

'Fire at will, men,' Anderson commanded, but when he saw that the aim of the others was not as accurate at such a range and that the troopers had jumped from their horses to take cover behind rocks in the grass or under the wagon, he shouted, 'To horse, men.'

When they were all a'saddle Anderson raised his flashy carbine and cried, 'Charge!' leading them at a gallop down the slope to swerve around their prize, firing at any bluebelly in sight. The shots flashed and rattled back and forth as the soldiers replied.

'This ain't a good idea,' Sims groaned. It was bad enough trying to stay in the saddle without attempting to take aim and fire at the same time. It was all very well for these experienced gunmen but he was a civilian for God's sake! He had half a mind to fall off and surrender when old Skeeter's horse went tumbling head over heels and his rider rolled from his saddle. When he got to his feet Skeeter had lost his rifle and seemed too groggy to go for his sidearm. The troopers riddled him with bullets.

'Jeez!' Randy changed his mind: to surrender would be suicide.

Anderson urged his troops on, but even Baines seemed reluctant to get in too close. They were sitting ducks for the soldiers down in the grass. Lead buzzed and whined about their heads as the attack lost its impetus. Young Mace charged in and was lucky not to be hit. Anderson had emptied his carbine to little effect and pulled his revolver. But, as a bullet ripped through the sleeve of his uniform, there was a look of anguish on his face.

'Retreat, men,' he screamed. 'Retreat. Let's get out of here.'

It was bitter cordial for the southern renegades as, followed by the troopers' jeers, they charged off and headed for the Wichita mountains and lakes many miles away.

★　★　★

The two bounty hunters made their way south-east swinging past Apache Lake, French Lake, Fish Lake and Lost Lake until they reached the perfect turquoise pool of Crater Lake, a snowy mountain peak mirror-imaged on its surface.

'I figure we're too far south,' Clarke said. 'We'll head up this creek.'

At noon they paused to brew up coffee and watched beaver swimming busily back and forth building a dam of larch poles. 'It's sweet to see the critters coming back,' Cass mused. 'They were nearly wiped out by all them years of hunting.'

'Yeah, gents don't go in for them beaver top hats no more. Such is the fickleness of fashion. These busy animals allus make me feel positively lazy. Come on, boy, let's move.'

They emerged on to another valley with a wall of mountains to the north and, as they crossed it, encountered a pack of feathered Indians cantering towards them dragging a dead buffalo on a travois. Old attitudes died hard and both men loosened the sixguns on their belts. But most tribes in the Nations knew better than to court trouble these days. Jim greeted them with a raised palm of peace sign. They had blankets around their shoulders and fringed leggings. They pulled in their painted ponies. They had been hunting a small herd of buffalo — a few of the last still living, but, unlike the white man, would make use of every part, meat, hide, horns, even the gut and sinews.

'We look for white man, long white hair, goat beard, tall hat, caped coat.' Clarke tried to describe Anderson with sign language. 'You seen him? Any idea where Ketch Lake is.'

'Crazy man,' one of them said. 'We don't want him here.' He pointed along the valley. 'Ketch Lake! Cabin 'long there.'

His friends seemed more interested in the Palomino, one of them offering six ponies in exchange. 'No way,' Cass grinned. 'She's mine.'

There didn't seem to be anybody at home as they arrived at the cabin. No smoke. No horses. No tracks. The door was padlocked. Clarke kicked it in.

'Might as well make ourselves at home,' Jim said, poking around.

There was nothing of much moment apart from a crate of ammunition, a barrel of oats for the horses, stale-smelling blankets on the bunks and a bottle marked 'Poison'.

'Charming,' Cass remarked. 'Wonder who they does with that? They don't seem to have been here for a while. Maybe they been and gone.'

'In that case we might as well quit.' Clarke waved his hand at the mountains to the south. 'There's a million and a quarter acres of prairie beyond those hills. Old Greer County, and on into Texas. We can wave goodbye to any reward. On t'other hand I got a hunch they ain't got here yet.'

He built a fire in the stove while Cass fed the horses some oats, hefted their saddles and packs inside and went out to split more logs. The sheriff had traded tobacco and beads for some thick slices of buffalo hump and it was soon crackling juicily on the hot stove. 'Cosy, ain't it?' he laughed, as they got stuck into the grub.

'What we gonna do if or when they arrive?'

'That, my young friend, will be up to you. You're gonna be outside keeping guard. The main aim is to get Anderson alive. He's the one with the big moolah on his head. You keep your popgun handy and aim for his shoulder or legs rather than to kill. The others, well, that's up to you.'

'What are you gonna do?'

'I'm gonna git some shut eye on that bunk. I'll take the graveyard watch.'

'Right.' Cass grabbed his Creedmore and a blanket. 'I'll give ya a shout about midnight.'

★ ★ ★

'Looks like we got visitors.' Colonel Anderson drew in his mount and surveyed the cabin on a promontory of the moonlit lake, the smoke trickling from the chimney, the horses outside. A tall fellow in a black shirt, a low-crowned black hat and black cowboy boots stepped out of the shadow, slapping his arms as if to keep warm.

'That's Whispering Rick,' Randy Sims said. 'Jawbone must be inside.'

'Yeah,' Anderson mused. 'Come on, men. I'm hungry as a starved wolf.'

Cass heard the jingle of harness, saw the four riders coming out of the darkness along the shore, heard one of them call.

'Hi,' he managed to croak, his heart banging as he backed away, found his Creedmore propped against the wall, and thumped its butt on the cabin door. He gave a casual wave of greeting. 'Where you boys been?'

'That's the question I want to put to you two,' Anderson replied gruffly until he suddenly realized his mistake, pulling his horse in hard as he looked into the dark, deathly hole of the Creedmore. 'What the hell!'

'Yeah,' Cass gritted out. 'Throw up your hands, boys. I'm a lawman and calling on y'all to surrender. My associate's got you covered from up in the rocks.'

'A likely story.' Anderson went for the

big revolver under his coat, but without hesitation Cass fired, his bullet hitting his shoulder and knocking him from the saddle.

'You bastard!' Mace screamed, held his Colt .45, arm out-stretched and took aim to fire. But at that instant the cabin window shutter was smashed open and the .41's manstopper bullet ploughed right through the youth's chest and whistled past Randy's head. 'Chris'sakes!' Sims yelled, shooting up his hands. 'I surrender.'

Josiah Baines leaped from his mustang and scrambled away into the dark pursued by their gunshots.

'Where's that crafty monkey gotten to?' Clarke roared, bursting out of the cabin. 'Take a look round the back. Shoot on sight.' Cass prowled back around the cabin, standing in the dark shadows, peering up at the rocks. All he heard was the howl of a timber wolf out in the night. 'Where'n hell's he gawn?' he muttered.

A thin wire was suddenly noosed

around his neck from behind and jerked tight, razoring into his throat. Automatically he fired his gun, trying to direct it at his attacker behind. But the wire was cutting off his air. He flailed his arms, hopelessly, blacking out, feeling himself slumping to the ground.

'Sleep sweet,' a voice whispered.

'Cass.' Jim Clarke stepped out from the side of the cabin, saw a shadowy figure. 'Is that you?'

The answer was a burst of gunpowder flame as a bullet creased Jim's neck. He jumped back, breathing hard, then tried again, stepping out and fanning a volley of shots into the darkness.

Warily, he stepped forward and almost tripped over the young Texan. There was a scrambling sound and a whinnying of a horse. He dashed back to the front of the cabin and saw Baines a'straddle the bucking bare back of the Palomino, slashing at its hide with a wire loop, hanging on to its rope hackamore, and careering away out along the bank of the lake.

Clarke fired his last bullet from the Thunderer at him but it was a futile gesture. 'Hot damn,' he said, checking that Anderson was no threat, quickly frisking him, relieving him of a knife and small pocket pistol.

There was blood staining the cloth of Anderson's coat at the shoulder and he was whining about his legal rights. 'Aw, shut up.' Clarke stomped his boot into his face and kicked him in the crotch. 'You make another squeak you'll get the full treatment.'

He eyed Sims, who still had his hands high, then went to take a look at Cass. Was he dead, or was he alive?

11

Josiah Baines rode the golden-coated Palomino wildly through the moonlit night, following the string of glimmering lakes, spurring and quirting the mare cruelly, guiding her with the hackamore and the pressure of his knees, riding bareback like an Indian. On and on he went, cursing the two men who had dared destroy their scheme. He was on his own now. He would go north, collect the cash from the cave, disappear into No Man's Land where others of his ilk hung out . . .

The sun was rising, firing the sky in the east with a ruddy glow as he headed towards the opening of the Washita valley. Suddenly he spied a pitched-roof cabin, set back among the dark pines. He needed food for himself and saddle and bridle for the horse. He turned off the trail and saw a tall young woman herding cows into a field. A three-legged hound came running at him, barking shrilly. He whipped it out of the way.

'Waal, I do declare, what a purty sight at this time of the marnin',' he crooned, as he drew alongside and eyed her long, bare legs, lasciviously. 'As fine a female specimen of the white race as I ever did see. Howdy, gal, you got any spare horses in this place?'

'No.' Audrey turned her green eyes on him and shivered with fear, knowing there was devilment in this man. 'We don't have none. Where did you get *that* one?'

'You like her? A fine ride. Some feller sold her to me yesterday. He didn't have use for her no more. I need to rest her up a coupla hours. That allows time for you an' me to get acquainted. You like havin' fun with strangers?'

'No, I don't,' she cried. 'Where is he, that fella who owned the horse? What have you done with him?'

'Oh,' Baines drawled, smiling at her in an eerie way. 'I do believe he's dead. Waal, what did he expect, trying to kill me an' the colonel like that?'

'He's dead? Cass?' She stared at him as if unable to take in the information. 'You killed him?'

'That's what I said. Was that his name? Heavens to Betsy! Don't tell me you were sweet on that boy. How sad.' Josiah grinned and reached out to stroke her cheek, or, perhaps, more. She jumped away, sprinting back to the cabin.

'Yeah, run, you lanky witch,' Baines laughed. 'You ain't gonna escape from me so easy.'

He rode up to the cabin and vaulted down cheerily. 'She musta gone and hid inside. Bless the child, she likes to play little games.' He hitched the horse and stretched his wiry limbs as Mr Cox came outside. 'Good marnin' to you, suh. I've just been conversing with the gal, assumedly your daughter. I've been riding hard all night. Any chance of refreshment in your household?'

John Wesley Cox eyed the sweated-up Palomino. 'That horse needs a rub-down. You'll find hay for it in the barn.'

'All in good time.' He pushed past the old man as if he owned the place. 'First I need feeding, myself.'

Inside the cabin a neat little woman in a long dress was standing anxiously watching and waiting. Audrey was holding a musket pointed at the intruder. 'Get out!' she cried. 'Or I'll shoot you. I will.'

'Is that a pleasing welcome for a weary man? You Yankees don't have much hospitality.' He ignored her, poking past into the kitchen. 'All I'm asking for is a mug of coffee, a plate of vittles and some kindness.'

Audrey desperately fiddled with the hammer of the musket. It seemed to be stuck. She had never fired the piece before, but now she was determined to. This man meant harm to them.

Baines spun round on his boot-heel, grabbed hold of the barrel and wrenched the weapon from her. Cox had stepped back into the cabin. 'You shouldn't let your daughter have charge of such a dangerous weapon. An ol' cap 'n ball, huh? I do believe she don't know how to handle it. She needs teaching a lesson.'

'You're going too far, sir.'

'How do you git these idle wimminfolk to look after a man's needs around here? I'm in need of some grub.' Josiah ensconced himself on a stool at the table, leaned back against the wall, raised his voice and roared, 'Git damn well cookin', you bitches.'

'No need for that.' John Wesley's voice quavered as he leaned on his walking stick. 'Cook him up some ham and eggs, Elisabeth. Then he will be on his way.'

'Oh, Elisabeth, is it? How about t'other one?'

'Audrey,' Cox replied, quietly. 'You leave her alone.'

'Why? Would she be one of them innocent types I've heard about? Not many of them these days.' Baines reached up and took one of John Wesley's few precious, leather-bound volumes from a shelf. 'I see you are a scholar, sir. What's this? Horace. Never heard of him.' He tossed it across the floor. 'All such philosophizing is a little beyond me. I'm just a simple Southern boy.'

'Indeed?' Cox muttered, retrieving the book, clutching it to him like a miser his gold.

The mocking tone of Baines's one-way conversation continued as he chomped through his breakfast. The three inhabitants of the cabin stood and stared at him, occasionally glancing at each other.

Josiah swilled down his coffee, eructated loudly, got to his feet and said, 'Now to see to my horse. Audrey will help me, won't you, Audrey?'

'No!' Elisabeth screamed. 'Leave her be. I beg you. She's not — '

Baines struck her a back-hander across her jaw, sending her crashing to the floor. 'I warn you, mister, don't try anythang. I am a merciful man but I have my limits.' He took hold of Audrey's upper arm in what could only be termed a grip of steel. 'I won't detain this gal long, then I will ride on my way.'

'You won't.' John Wesley raised his gnarled walking stick containing a barrel and simple, if ancient firing piece, a poacher's gun he had brought with him from England. 'No, sir.'

The gun exploded, deafeningly, but it was not the most accurate of armaments. The ball smashed into the wall as Baines whipped out his revolver and fired. Mr Cox hurtled back and lay groaning, holding his bloody thigh, on the floor.

'I oughta kill ya. But you're lucky. I'm short of ammunition. With any luck you'll bleed to death.'

He crouched, one hand on knee, foul-breathed and grinning into John Wesley's face. 'Let me explain what I plan to do to your daughter.' In a hoarse croak he detailed his obscene plans. He got to his feet. 'Come 'long, girl. No time to waste.' He grabbed her by the hair and dragged her out of the cabin. 'Quit that squawkin'. Bring that horse.'

Audrey unhitched the Palomino, grimacing as the hand tore at her hair. She dragged the mare along with them, her mind filled with exploding thoughts of escape. But she knew if she tried he would kill her.

'Rub it down.' Baines released her in the barn. 'Give it some corn. Come on, jump to it. I ain't got all day.'

He kicked some straw into a heap to make a comfortable bed and watched her at her tasks. 'Right. Come here.'

'No.' Audrey shied like a stubborn horse, poised to flee, but he stood between her and the doorway. There was a pitchfork propped in a corner. 'No, please, mister, I don't want to.'

'Come here.' He pounced and grappled with her, tearing her dress half from her body, twisting her down on to the heap and thrusting himself upon her. 'No!' she screamed.

* * *

'Where am I? Where's my hat?' were Cass's first words when he struggled out of unconsciousness.

'Is that all a Texan thinks of?' Jim had guffawed as he kneeled over him. 'That's a nasty red cut round your neck. I've been slapping your face tryin' to bring you round for half an hour.'

'Yeah?' Cass's voice was a husky whisper. 'He tried to throttle me.'

'I better attend to my other patient now. He ain't hurt too bad. His revolver deflected my shot.'

Clarke had helped Cass back into the cabin. 'At least we got ourselves one big fish to take back for his hanging.'

'My attorney will hear about this, Sheriff.' Anderson was grovelling on the floor, clutching at himself. 'Torture and abuse of a prisoner. This is against all humanitarian concepts.'

'Shut up. You want me to patch up your shoulder or not? First, though, you're gonna tell me what you done with all that loot?'

'Never. You won't see a cent of it.'

'Oh, yeah?' Clarke booted him again. 'You'll be crying like a baby soon.'

'I know where it is,' Sims put in. 'I'll lead you there if you put in a word for me.'

'Sometimes I feel that I'm doing the Lord's bidding — ridding this country of degenerate filth so that decent folk can go about their honest lives in peace and friendship,' the sheriff mused. 'What the hell you think I can do for you?'

'Tell the judge at the trial I've helped out. I'll turn state's evidence. I didn't know this guy was crazy. I've gotta do my time, I know. All I ask is you recommend that I do it at Riker's Island. Then my poor old mother in New York can visit me before she passes away. She ain't too good. Besides, they do better grub there.'

'Where's the other one?' Cass had

asked, coming to his senses.

'He's hightailed it, I'm sorry to say on your horse.'

'What?' Cass sprang to his feet. 'I'm going after him. I'll take your horse. You can have his. Or his.'

'Hold it.' But Clarke's words were too late. The Texan had gone.

*   *   *

It was early morning. There was a distinct trail on the frosty grass and it was heading towards the Cox's cabin. Cass's heart sank as he rode in. There was a shrill scream from the barn and a man's angry words. 'Bite me, would yuh, you vixen. Agh!'

Cass swung from the horse, leaped into the stable and saw a man over the girl, lambasting her with swinging punches. 'You — I'll fillet you like a stinking herring.'

Audrey was kicking and struggling. Cass spotted the pitchfork. He picked it up and stuck it with all his strength into

Baines's back. 'Howja like some of your own treatment?'

Josiah squealed like a stuck rat, twisting round, breaking free, grabbing his sixgun to aim and fire. Cass kicked it from his fist. And stuck the pitchfork into his gut, twisting it. He stood and watched him squirm as Audrey clambered to her feet, half-naked, her dress in shreds.

'Steady!' Cass caught hold of her, pulled her into him, wiped blood from her face.

'He is a bad man,' she stuttered. 'It is him stinks bad. He tried to make me . . . I didn't want to . . . I bit him hard. He tasted horrid.'

'Yeah, I bet he did. Well, he looks damn sorry for himself now.' Cass tightened his arm about her, stroked her bruised cheek. 'You did right. He can't hurt you no more.' He felt the wire-burn around his own neck. 'Nor me, neither.'

★　★　★

'Here y'are, kid.' Sheriff Clarke arrived about noon with his handcuffed prisoners on horseback. He tossed Cassius the Marlin carbine with its gold and silver inlays on the firing casing. 'The spoils of war. It was the colonel's. Now it's yours. He probably stole it, anyway.'

'That's a lie.' Anderson's shoulder wound was not as bad as it might have been, the Thunderer's powerful bullet passing through flesh without hitting bone. He had lost a good bit of blood and he was just feeling weak. However, he was not too weak to protest. 'I paid five hundred dollars for that piece. It's my personal property.'

'Wow!' Cass examined the carbine with delight. 'Mr Cox can have my ol' Creedmore now. When he gets well, that is. It'll be more use than that walking stick of his.'

'Why, what's been going on?' Sheriff Clarke dabbed the bullet crease across his neck with his bandanna. 'Don't tell

186

me. Has that rat Baines been up to his tricks?'

'You can say that again.' Cass filled him in on what had happened and led them into the cabin where Mr Cox was laid out on his bunk and Baines was manacled on the floor. Mrs Cox had washed the bleeding pitchfork wounds to his front and back and bound them with rags.

But Baines's pale eyes still glimmered with menace. 'You ain't won yet.'

'Listen to him!' Clarke bellowed with laughter. 'Don't know when he's beat.' The sheriff took off his big Stetson to reveal his gleaming white, bald dome that rarely saw the sun. 'Any chance of a bite to eat, Mrs Cox? I ain't had nuthin' yet. I s'pose I gotta feed these monkey's, too, to keep 'em alive for their hanging.'

'I was sorely tempted to kill that snake,' Cass said, 'but I heeded what you said, Sheriff. They're worth more alive than dead. Watch out for him. He's one of them rattlers who strikes when you ain't expecting it.'

Mrs Cox attended to her brother-husband, who was laid on his cot. 'I'm giving him some willow-bark tea. The Indians swear by it. I'm feared his leg might get blood-pizening.'

This was often the case with gunshot wounds. A man could linger for months before he succumbed. Clarke made a down-turned grimace. 'Just try to keep it clean. That's all you can do.'

'Right, I'll see what vittals I can rustle up. How about fried chicken, omelettes and beans?'

'That sounds fine,' Clarke beamed. 'Now you three, this is how it will be. It is strongly possible we will run into a cavalry patrol on the way back to Wichita town. From what Randy has told me about your stupid attack on the paymaster's wagon they'll be out combing the territory. So what's it to be? You want me to hand you over? You fancy a quick court martial, then being stuck up aginst the stockade wall and shot? Bang, bang. Goodbye, you three *amigos?* Agreed?'

'Probably true,' Anderson replied. 'What you want is to get us to Wichita town for any ree-wards?'

'You got it. So, your choice: me or the soldiers? You try your luck at Wichita courthouse you might avoid the noose if some lawyer gives 'em blarney. Twenty years' hard labour, nineteen if you get out on parole.'

'We'll come with you, Sheriff,' Anderson decided. 'What's your plan?'

'Simple. Firstly ye'll get outa them Confederate carnival costumes. I'll keep 'em for your grand arrival in Wichita. Mr Sims ain't wearing one, but he'd better ditch that derby. I called in at the trading store on the way here and bought ya new pants and jackets and three hats to make ya look more the part. Sims and Anderson, you'll be my deputies. Anderson, you got shot when we chased after and arrested this dangerous horse thief, Josiah. Here's a coupla tin stars I keep in my pack. You're deputized. Pin 'em on.'

He knocked Baines's Confederate cap off his cropped head and jammed a wide-brimmed one down on it. Then he bent down and jerked the yellow-striped pants off his bony legs. He did the same to Anderson, upending him on the floor in undignified fashion. 'Help 'em git these crazy jackets off, Cass. What's this?' he examined the insignia — 'Tenth Louisiana Brigade? Huh! Now for the rest of their disguises. Elisabeth, have you a pair of scissors?'

'Yes, in my sewing box. Here they are.'

'Thank you. Hold him down. He ain't gonna like this. His beautiful moustachio and his lovely long locks. Here we go. Hold him tight, Cass.'

'What?' Anderson spluttered his angry protests as the sheriff dumped himself down hard on his chest. 'Ouf!' He kicked out as Clarke brandished the scissors. 'You can't. How dare you? I'm a senior officer.'

'You sure are.' The sheriff grinned

sadistically as he went to with the scissors, tossing chunks of his white hair on to he floor. 'But nobody ain't gonna recognize you now. Careful, pal, you'll get your ears nicked. Now where's that cut-throat razor of mine? Time to give you a nice close shave.'

'No,' Anderson howled vainly as the sheriff beamed at him and snipped off his beard and moustache. 'I can't bear it.'

'You've shorn him like a sheep,' Elisabeth cried.

'I ain't finished yet. Stop wriggling, you tadpole.' Clarke scraped the razor across Anderson's jaws and pate until he looked like a peeled boiled egg. 'There y'are. Now where's that other varmint?'

'No!' Josiah cried, defiantly. 'You leave me 'lone.'

'Won't take a trice.' Clarke sawed through Baines's hedge-thick walrus danglers. 'They gotta go. They probably got your description.'

'You Yankees, you're vandals,' Josiah

whined as he was held down.

'Yeah, what you might call desecrating a Southern monument.'

When the sheriff had finished them, he manacled them with his cuff-irons to each other, and shoved them towards the table. 'Ah, food's up. Thank you, Mrs Cox. Dig in, boys. You got a rough ride ahead.'

Audrey had said little, sitting on a chair, a blanket around her, watching with her large, green, wondering eyes, wringing her hands on a 'kerchief, still visibly upset, or in shock. 'Are you going away?' she whispered to Cass. 'Will you come back?'

'Sure I will.' He tugged at her pony-tail. 'Look on the bright side, gal. I need to know you're rootin' for me.'

Clarke regarded her kindly, as he finished his meal and lit his corncob pipe. The Coxes had told the girl about her cradle-swap in order to be honest with her. 'Just think, Audrey, under other circumstances you would be a belle in the City of London doing the season, I think they call it, with maids and coaches, footmen and balls, diamonds and jewels and fancy dresses, waltzing around living the life of Riley. Funny, ain't it?'

'I don't want dresses and jewels. I don't want to go to London. I like it here.' She stared back at him, miserably. 'You ain't gonna *make* me, mister, are you?'

'No, course not, I'm just supposin'. You can stay here by all means.'

'What, in this lousy hovel?' Baines jeered. 'She's got bats flyin' in her attic, that one.'

'You shut up,' Cass butted in. 'This gal's got aristocratic blood. Look, you can tell by the jut of her nose' — he stroked it fondly — 'she's worth a million of any mongrel like you.'

'And one day, under Reconstruction, such decent folk will have a right to live here and make good use of this land,' the sheriff added, getting to his feet. 'Come on, cut the cackle. We gotta be on our way.'

12

It was good to be out in the early spring sunshine in Indian country. Cass savoured the scent of wild pine and sage as they rode north through the Washita valley under great white clouds in the pure blue sky. On one side at this point, the valley wall rose steep-sided to a cliff covered with ponderosas and from it a thin stream tumbled, a spray of haze boiling out of the falls below. On the far side he could see elk grazing in the shadows of some cottonwoods. 'I'd love to settle here,' he murmured.

'Well, boy, maybe you can,' the sheriff replied. 'Me, I'd rather be out on the prairie. We get these rewards I'll have the wherewithal to stock a fine ranch.'

'That young woman's cast a spell on me,' Cass said, 'same as this country has.'

'How about the one in Eureka?'

'She's OK. Now and again. We got the same sense of humour. I mean, she laughs at my jokes. But, as for runnin' off with her' — the image of Mary's three boys, the spitting likeness of her dour husband, and the thought of them staring accusingly at him for the rest of his life flashed into Cass's mind — '*and* her kids? It just ain't practical.'

'That ain't very gentlemanly to my mind.'

'No,' he said, glumly. 'I s'pose not. But you ain't me, Jim.'

★ ★ ★

They camped by the river that night. They tied their three prisoners to three separate lodgepole pines so they couldn't get up to mischief. 'Cain't we come closer to the fire?' Randy whined. 'I'm freezin' my butt off here.'

'Nope.' Jim warmed himself at the flames. 'I don't trust you monkeys.'

'This is a fine howdy-doo,' Colonel

Anderson muttered. 'How do we get out of this, Josiah?'

Baines, tied to the bole of the tree, his hands cuffed, his boots stuck out, grimaced with the pain of the pitchfork holes in his back and front. 'We been in worse, J.G. We bide our time. Our chance will come.'

'Yeah, some hope,' Randy remarked.

'You, you traitor,' Baines scowled. 'You'll be first on my revenge list.'

'I should never have trusted a Yankee,' Anderson remarked. 'This revolting little worm blabbed straight out about where the cash was hid. That was our retirement pension, Josiah. We've got to do something.'

'Ha!' Sims scoffed. 'What happened to the sacred cause?'

* * *

It was early the next morning as they came out of the Washita valley on to the prairie that they saw a column of cavalry, three abreast, the Stars and

196

Stripes fluttering at their head, pounding towards them. The sheriff reined in, quickly unlocked the colonel and Sims from their manacles, and raised one hand to greet the troopers. He pointed with his other to the tin star glinting on his chest. 'Howdy, boys,' he shouted as they came face to face. 'My name's Jim Clarke, Sheriff of Wichita town for many years. You may have heard of me.'

That morning Josiah Baines's condition had worsened so they had made a travois of larch poles to lay him on, pulled by Lop Ears while the other two prisoners rode by his side.

'These here are my three deputies, Cass Clacy, Randy Chowkowski, and Conrad van der Vort, who unfortunately took a bullet through the shoulder from the fella on the back there. As you can see, he's in a worse state.'

The officer in charge looked at them doubtfully and edged his mount past to inspect Baines. 'Who's he?'

197

Sheriff Clarke followed him. 'A lowdown cuss who killed a man over a game of cards in the Grand Central saloon. We came after him. Virgil Payne is his name. You heard of him?'

'No.' The young officer stroked his clean-shaven chin in thought. 'How long have you been on his trail?'

'Three long weeks. We're in a hurry to git back.'

'You seen anything of the so-called Rebel Raiders, the bunch of bank robbers? They attacked our wagon, killed one of our troopers.'

'Rebel Raiders? You mean they've been on the rampage while we've been out? Holy pigshit! This is news to me. We ain't seen nobody 'cept Injins fer days. God's teeth, I sure *better* get back!'

The captain rode back and took another look at Anderson and Sims. They sat their mounts, wide-brimmed hats pulled over their eyes, hunched in their jackets and bandannas, guns on hips, emptied of bullets but the captain wasn't to know. With tin stars on their chests they looked like real lawmen to him.

'He's telling the truth,' a trooper sang out. 'He's the sheriff of Wichita. I seen him there patrolling the saloons. Would recognize that bruiser any day.'

'Right, do you want to bring these men into the infirmary at Fort Reno for treatment, Sheriff?'

'I'm OK. No need to,' Anderson growled, saluting the flag. 'God bless Old Glory! God bless America! God bless you, sir!'

'We ain't bothered about that cur on the stretcher,' Jim said, 'whether he lives or dies, but we wanna try an' get him back alive for his hanging.'

When the captain had saluted, ordering the cavalry to ride on Jim said, 'You were over-acting a bit there weren'tcha, Anderson?'

The morose southern colonel rarely smiled, but for once his embittered face cracked into a grin. 'We fooled 'em, didn't we?'

'Stick your wrists out. I'm cuffing you again.'

*　*　*

'There it is.' Randy led them to the cave and lit a lantern inside illuminating its pale alabaster walls. He hauled away a covering of rocks beneath which was Anderson's war chest of brass-bound oak.

The sheriff found the key on the colonel and opened up. 'My God!' he muttered, as he examined the gold and silver coins and stacks of greenbacks. He did a quick count, a thousand dollars in each pack, apart from the coins. Ten packs, ten thousand dollars.

'How we gonna get this back?' Cass asked.

'We ain't. Randy here reckons that apart from them two outside nobody else knows of this cave apart from a few Indians. We'll leave the bulk of it here until I've negotiated a big cut for ourselves with the banks for its return.

It's gonna take some time. I'm gonna need it in writing and the agreement in an attorney's hands. Never trust a shifty banker. They're the slimiest toads who ever walked God's earth.'

'What about the rewards?'

'We'll negotiate them separately.'

'Whoo!' Cass ran his fingers through the coin, tested with his teeth a golden double eagle, worth twenty dollars. 'There's a fortune.'

'Don't get gold fever, boy, or any ideas of splitting for California with it.' Clarke's hand went to the staghorn grip of his .41, and he stepped back, a grim look in his worn eyes. 'Gold does funny things to men, even men like you, Clacy.'

'You wouldn't?' The Texan's eyes narrowed as he met the older man's. 'We got to stick together, Jim. I ain't figuring on riding the wrong side of the law. And I don't reckon you are, either.'

'If I had to, I *would* do. Shoot you without hesitation. But you're right.' He stuck out his hand to shake. 'You're made of the right stuff, pal. I ain't planning on crossing the line and I don't believe you are either.'

'No,' Cass grinned at him. 'How long before we get a share on a chunk of this?'

'Shouldn't be too long. We've got a lever. Go git that carpet bag from the pack on the mule. We're in the money, boy. We'll take five hundred in coin just to prove we ain't joking.'

They filled the bag with the gold and roped it beneath the tarpaulin on the mule and went on their way, Josiah Baines groaning and luridly cursing at every bump in the prairie.

'Them vultures are circling.' Cass nodded towards the big birds soaring on thermals in the sky. 'They musta smelled Baines's blood.'

'It's the human vultures we got to worry about,' Clarke gritted out.

When they reached a bluff as they neared the Canadian River the Palomino began to fidget and tremble again. Cass looked up and saw a huge grizzly, ten-feet or more tall on his hind legs, peering at them. 'Jeez! You got your shotgun ready, Jim?'

'If he charges we'll dump Josiah. He can have him for supper.'

As they eased their mounts past nervously, the fearsome bear went back to exploring under a dead log he'd overturned. It was another reminder of why a man needed to carry his heavy weapons at readiness when he rode through the wilderness as a protection against predators, both animals and human.

They were glad to reach the bank of the river and made a successful crossing. This time it was Baines on his stretcher who half-drowned and came up spluttering. For some reason it seemed to amuse his companions.

They crossed the Cimarron and the Great Salt Plain and late one evening as a tempest of snow swept down from the north reached Ponca City again. They dumped Anderson and Baines, cuffing them to iron mangers in the stable at the rear, unsaddled the animals and went to take a look. 'You can come with us,' Clarke told the tubby little Sims. 'But one false move and you won't be seeing your mama again.'

When Cass held up a double eagle between two fingers at the door grille Ponca Bob opened up swiftly.

'You got any eats? We got two other guests out back.'

The joint was filled with a veritable international assortment: a Mexican in sombrero, with vicious rowelled spurs, the German farmer, a black ex-slave in a top hat and fancy vest, a Chinese coolie off the railroad, an Irish navvy and a couple of dark-jowled Anglo drifters, their eyes as cold as the night sky. Most of them were gathered around the roulette wheel. Stale sweat and body grease gave them the smell of animals, mingled with tobacco and whiskey fumes.

'You had good huntin', boys?' Ed Collins, in a dirt-brown hat and suit that had seen better days, stood over them as they sat around the stove and got stuck in to game soup and beans. Thin lips in a hatchet face bared yellow teeth. 'Who's he?' He nodded at Sims crouched on his stool. 'Your prisoner or your pal?'

'Go stick your nose somewhere else,' Jim growled.

Collins gave a cackle and lurched away.

'Don't much like the looks of him,' Randy squeaked as he sucked up his soup. 'Who is he?'

'The sorriest critter along the creek,' Jim replied. 'He ain't never done a day's honest work in his life.'

'He's sure got the sneaky looks of some sheep-killin' dog,' Cass remarked, as he watched Collins slip outside. 'I better go keep an eye on our boys an' our gold. Randy, can you bring 'em some grub?'

'Sure,' Sims called. 'Take it easy, pal.'

* * *

'Waal, I'll be my gran' pappy's maiden aunt,' Ed Collins crooned, as he struck a match and lit a lantern. 'You two ain't the fry I expected to see in the pan.'

'Shut up, and listen,' Colonel Anderson snapped, as he sprawled on the stable floor chained to the iron manger grid. 'Set us free and you will be well-rewarded.' He glanced at the carpet bag. 'I know where a goodly amount of gold is hid not far from here. You have the word of a southern gentleman it is yours if you get us out of here.'

'Who are you?' Collins whined in his nasal drawl. 'I had the idea they was bringing in them Raiders.'

'They have, you fool. We are they. Look alert, you idiot.'

Collins heard Cass's footsteps. Cass had paused to buy a jug of whiskey planning to dose the maggots in Baines's wounds with part of it.

'What you doing here? The sheriff told you to git.'

'Oh, Jim and I go back a long way,'

Collins sniggered. 'He often jests.'

'What were you talking about?'

'What you think he was talking about, dimwit?' A big, burly man had stepped out of the darkness, put a hand on his shoulder, spun him round and the whiskey went spinning as he smashed a fist into his mouth. 'Remember me?'

As Cass rocked on his feet the man headbutted him, knocking him to the ground. He bent over and breathed foul air into Cass's face. 'Mary confessed everything after I beat it outa her. All them dirty thangs you two got up to in the afternoon. You should be ashamed.'

'Bill?' Cass had a silly idea he'd said this before. 'What you doing here? I thought you were laid up.'

'Yeah, well, my leg healed real quick. You done well, Deputy Clacy. You got your men. Seems like they know where the cash is hid. So I'm taking over duty from you.' Bill Molineux smirked down at him as Cass began climbing groggily to his feet. 'Oh, you want some more?'

He crunched his hamfist into the cowboy's face splattering blood and a tooth.

Clacy gasped with pain. Lights were exploding in his brain. His blood was up and he went crazy swinging a volley of wild haymakers at Molineux. But most of the blows went wild. Bill was twice the weight of him and he dodged, deflected and attacked, pincering Cass in a mighty bearhug, headbutting him again, to the nose this time, and jeered as he collapsed on top of Anderson. 'Strike a superior officer, would you?'

'Get off of me,' the colonel growled. 'You're beaten, son.'

The Texan was struggling to his feet again. He ducked a swinger from Molineux as Ed picked up a wooden pole and swung it at Cass. He missed and nearly hit Bill, instead. But on the reverse swing he caught Cass hard across the temple, felling him.

'He's out for the count,' Collins said. 'Did you hear that clunk? Like splitting a coconut.'

Molineux put his finger to his lips for they could hear the crunch of Jim Clarke's boots on the snow. As he stepped into the barn Clarke saw Molineux and went for his Colt. Ed swung like a baseball champ again and cracked the back of the sheriff's cranium. He went down, poleaxed. 'Got him,' Collins cried. 'What shall I do? Kill 'em?'

'No,' Bill commanded. 'I wouldn't kill a fellow law officer. Break their legs. Put 'em outa action like I was. See if they like a taste of that.'

Ed giggled and went to with a will, cracking the pole across the unconscious lawmen's legs. Randy had put his nose through the door, watching horrified.

'Come in, Shorty,' Bill beckoned. 'Come and jine us. Who are you?'

'He's with us,' Anderson said. 'Get the sheriff's keys. Free us. We'll go halves on the cash we got.'

'No,' Bill said. 'Here's the deal. First, where's that gold you were talking about? You give us that, then we take you three in, claim the rewards. I'll lodge you in Eureka jail. But once I've got the reward cash you'll break out of jail and lead me to the rest of the loot. Where is it and how much?'

'Ten grand in gold and used notes,' the colonel replied, airily. 'It's hidden not far past the Canadian River. Why not go back now and we can all head for Texas?'

'No. I'm sticking to my plan.' Bill had found the keys and released them, then cuffed Anderson to Sims. He eyed Baines. 'What's the matter with him? Can he ride?'

'I don't know. He ain't too good.'

'Well, he'll have to. I ain't hanging about. Now where's that gold nearby you talked about?'

'You're practically standing on it.'

Ed Collins grabbed the carpet bag and pulled it open. 'Hey-diddley-dee! Just look at this. He ain't lying.'

'Bring it. You three can ride them mustangs. They got more stamina than that circus horse. He can keep it. Snap to it,' Bill commanded. 'Let's git outa here.'

Maybe it had been a false spring, but icy tempests from the frozen north could sweep down across the central prairies up until as late as May. However, the sudden storm had swept on its way leaving a crisp white helmet of snow across the prairie. The moon glinted down on the bare landscape guiding them on their way. At dawn they paused by a stand of pines on a rough outcrop of rocks to give their mustangs a rest and kindled a fire to boil their coffeepot. Baines sank to the ground, his face grimly showing the agony of his damaged insides. His stretcher had been abandoned and riding was hard. But a man who had endured ten years in the hell of Yuma prison was not one to complain. He even forced a grin at Anderson. 'That

★

211

sure was a pleasure, J.G., to see them two beaten to pulp.'

Bill Molineux glanced at a saddle-back of purple hills as the sun beyond flashed its first rays as if struggling to rise and told Ed and his prisoners, 'Ain't far to Caldwell now.'

Ed prowled behind him as if to avoid the wind-drifting smoke and the next thing Bill knew his Colt had been whipped from his holster. 'Don't make a move, Bill. You can have them three for the reewards. I ain't going back.'

Collins snatched up the carpet bag of coin. 'This'll do me. That's fair, ain't it?'

Bill roared like a grizzly and struggled to his feet, his bad leg still stiff, heading towards Ed as he backed away waggling the revolver. 'Stay back,' Ed cried. 'I'll shoot. I will.'

'You piece of shit,' Bill shouted. 'You ain't going nowhere.'

Collins panicked, backing away right up to a well-like hole beneath the trees. Suddenly his boots slipped on the ice and with a yelp of fear he crashed backwards down into the hole. There was an ominous warning rattle and he screamed as the snake struck, ejecting poison from its fangs. Molineux peered down into the rocks and roots and saw Collins on his back among a writhing nest of serpents, his screams fading as he succumbed. He was still clutching the carpet bag to his chest. 'You can keep it. And the gun. I got my carbine.' Molineux gave a whistle of disbelief. 'That's what they call the Wages of Sin. I sure ain't going down there.'

★ ★ ★

Jim Clarke blinked awake into consciousness and gasped with pain. His big fists were manacled to the iron horse manger, above his head as he lay on the stable floor. 'My leg's broken,' he groaned.

Cassius Clacy was chained to a separate manger nearby. This was no Indian construction. The curved iron had been solidly bolted into deeply embedded oak posts years before when the stable had been a backwoodsman's trading store.

Cassius feared at first that his leg, too, was broken it was so painful. But, no. 'Mine's OK. I can move it.' He spat blood from his puffed-up lips and squinted at Clarke through a half-closed eye. 'Ed Collins didn't finish his job on me. He musta been in too much of a hurry to get away. Not that my legs are a lot of good to me. We ain't gettin' out of this in a hurry.'

'I shoulda known that crab-louse Collins was up to something. We walked right into their trap. I'll *kill* 'em when I catch up.'

Ponca City didn't boast a farrier's forge. They rode their ponies unshod hereabouts. 'I doubt if anybody's got such a thang as a file,' Cass sang out. 'We're stuck fast.'

They lay on the stable floor listening to the hullabaloo from Ponca Bob's cabin. Nobody was aware of their plight or would hear if they yelled. Cass lay for some time and worried at his manacles. Suddenly his long fingers and slender wrists wriggled free as he gritted his remaining teeth against the searing pain. 'Jeez,' he gasped, soothing them.

Clarke, however, was stuck fast. 'I'll go find Bob,' Cass called, as he staggered away.

'You boys have plenty fun, huh?' The Indian grinned at them, but after promise of reward if he cared for Jim he found a couple of splints, straightened and wrapped tight his leg. 'You not go nowhere for while, 'less we chop off hands.'

'No need for that. I'll be back.' Cass buckled on Rick's shiny Smith & Wessons, saddled the Palomino, hauled himself aboard and rode off into the dawn light.

The trail of hoofprints was easy to follow across the snow-glistening prairie. When he reached the rocky bluff he found scuffed prints around the remains of their fire. One set led away as if a man had walked backwards to a rocky edge of cliff followed by normal bootmarks.

Where they terminated Cass looked over into a deep hole and saw Ed sprawled at the bottom amid a seething nest of rattlers. There was something ghastly about the way he clutched the carpet bag, about his staring eyes.

Cass shuddered, mounted up, and went on his way.

* * *

He rode into Caldwell later that day and, as if to welcome him, saw Josiah Baines swinging in the fierce prairie wind from the hoist of a grain store, a rawhide rope taut around his throat. His eyes bulged and his mouth gaped as if in a final cry of defiance.

The widowed and raped storekeeper had put up a reward of $500 on Baines's head and had had her revenge. It seemed Bill Molineux had traded Josiah in and had pocketed the cash.

'We don't waste time around here with fancy trials,' a man informed him. 'That deputy feller kept hold of them two others and took train up to Wichita.'

★ ★ ★

Molineux was boasting to a crowd in the Grand Central saloon of how he had been ambushed by Jawbone and Whispering Rick and shot them both down, leaving them dead in the Indian Nations, and how he had captured the other three single-handed and brought them back to Kansas for justice. 'I ain't yet recovered the stolen cash but I'm working on it,' he yelled, knocking back whiskey amid his admirers at the bar.

Cass Clacy limped in, bloody and dishevelled and his voice rang out, 'That's a lie.'

They all turned to stare at him. 'What d'ye mean?' Deputy Zach Stevens demanded.

'Your own sheriff, Jim Clarke, will tell

you that we killed Jawbone and Rick and brought those other three in, at least as far as Ponca City.' Cass pushed through the crowd who parted for him and took a stance along the bar from Molineux, hitching back his buckskin jacket from the ivory-handled revolvers on his hips. 'This turnip head and his no-good sidekick, Ed Collins, jumped us there, near kicked the life outa us and broke Jim's leg. Ain't that so, Bill? Maybe you shoulda made a proper job of it. Maybe now's your chance.'

'Rubbish,' Bill blustered, his fingers reaching for the new ten-dollar Colt he had bought himself. 'This kid's jealous of me. It's him who's spouting lies. You don't believe him, do ya?'

'The best way for us to find out is to go down right now to Ponca City,' Zach cried, 'and see what Sheriff Clarke's got to say.'

'Aw, they've concocted this rubbish between 'em. I'm taking my prisoners and heading back to Eureka. And nobody ain't gonna stop me.'

'Ain't they?' Cass eased his fingers and licked his bruised lips, nervously, as the crowd began to shuffle back out of the way of flying lead.

It was just as well they did for Bill had his gun out first, but, as he fired, Maggie McGinty hit him on the head with her parasol and his bullet went wild, smashing bottles and glasses on the bar.

'You bladder of lard. Arrest me, would you, loudmouth!' She danced around him jabbing the pointed end of the scarlet brolly at his belly as he turned to fight her off. '*Gardez-la!*'

'Keep away, you fiend,' Molineux roared, trying to bat her off and fire at Cass at the same time.

Again his bullets whistled wide, smashing a window this time. Suddenly there was an ominous click. All his lead had gone.

Cass smiled, coldly, gripped both ivory handles, bringing them out to fire simultaneously aiming at his legs and his knees, making Molineux dance as bullets thudded into the floor. Maggie shrieked with laughter at his panicked antics.

Blue gunsmoke drifted as the audience and Molineux all seemed to hold their breath. Bill stood there, wide-eyed, wondering what Cass was going to do with the remaining bullets in the cylinder. 'Go on then,' he roared. 'Get on with it. Ain't ya gonna kill me?'

'Aw, you ain't worth killing. Anyway, you're my fellow deputy. I've no wish to kill you, yellow dog though you are.' He holstered the .44s and put an arm around Maggie's waist as she hugged him. 'How about I buy all you folks a drink? Give me a sarsparilla, barman. I'm teatotal from here on, myself.'

'You're joking!' Maggie cried.

'Nope. True. I got myself another gal and I'm a one woman man now. But,' he grinned, 'seein' as you just saved my life I'm gonna buy you a drink and pay your fine when I git back to Eureka.'

13

Cass looked quite the dude in his low-crowned deadman's hat, his newly laundered black shirt, silver flashing black boots and hip-hugging jeans, double-rigged with the ivory-handled .44s. He felt good, too, after a shave and hair trim, washing away the woodsmoke stink and easing his bruised body in a hot tub. He fondled Guinevere's mane as he checked her harness and stuck the flashy five hundred bucks carbine into her boot.

So happened Bill Molineux staggered out of some seedy rooming-house, unshaven and bleary-eyed, after drowning his sorrows the night before as he tried to forget his humiliation in front of the Wichita crowd. The town jailer had adamantly refused to give up possession of Anderson and Sims.

He came face to face with Cass, his

jaw dropping. 'Huh? Think you're a bigshot now.'

'You know, Bill, I was planning on giving you half of whatever rewards Jim gives me as your share.'

'What? I don't want your damn money.' Bill scowled at him. 'Go to hell.'

'I'm still willing to. I got a very forgiving nature. After all, you are my partner and you've got a feisty wife and three kids to support.'

'Don't try to be funny. What? You mean — '

'Sure,' Cass grinned, revealing the gap left by his missing tooth. 'Why not? You saved me a trip to the dentist. That one was a real pain. If you still want it I'll tell Jim to send half of my cut on to you.'

'You're joking?' Molineux looked perplexed. 'You will?'

'Of course the catch is, Jim's sworn to kill you so he might not agree.'

'Oh, I admit I went over the top.' Bill stuck out his chest getting back some of his braggart ways. 'But you know how it is. Man gets carried away.'

'Maybe if you'd fought fair I mighta given you as good as you gave. But, like you say, all's fair in love and war.'

'Love? War? Yeah. You could say that.' Bill stuck out his hand. 'Shake on it. I'm glad you feel this way.'

'I'm going back to Eureka to give in my badge. You want to ride along?'

'Sure.' Both men swung on to their broncs and clipped away out of town. 'Why, you had a better offer?'

'You could say so,' Cass mused. 'Met a Wichita angel I'm mighty keen to see again.'

'No? You mean that Mollie McGinty. Or some other dirty whore?'

'No,' Cass shouted, as he put Guinevere into a high-stepping trot. 'A real Wichita angel way down south among the lakes and mountains of the Wichita nation.'

★ ★ ★

Mary was at her cash box at the end of the bar in the Red Garter, her body trembling with excitement as she looked along at the sharp-faced gambler in his natty clothes who had breezed into town to rook the locals of their hard-earned cash. In her new green velvet dress she left the desk and strolled along behind the bar, giving him a sensual smile. 'Where are you from, handsome?'

'Oh, here and there.' The gold pin shone in his cravat, and his crafty eyes gleamed like a jackdaw's. 'Maybe you and I could get together 'fore I ride on?'

'Maybe.' Mary's eyes sparkled and she was about to agree when Bill and Cass burst through the saloon doors. 'What?' She gasped with surpise. 'What you two doing back?'

'What do you mean, woman?' Bill roared. 'My pal Cass here did all the work for me. I'm back here because I live and work here. I'm back to see my wife and boys and I'm starving. So you and me'll be heading home. What the devil d'ye mean, what am I doin' here?'

When he went out back to relieve himself, Mary glanced at the gambler in his fancy waistcoat and frockcoat with satin lapels. He was expertly shuffling a deck of cards. 'I . . . ah . . . look Cass, I've got to tell you, we can't go on like before.'

The Texan turned to the gambler who smiled at him, pocketed his pack and strolled along to join in a game. These were the words Cass had thought he would have difficulty putting to *her*. 'Ah, God,' he groaned, somewhat theatrically, slapping his forehead. 'I see I got competition. What am I gonna do?'

She frowned at him.' You been in a fight?'

'Yeah, Bill beat me up. But I don't hold a grudge. Hope I ain't interrupted anything?'

'No! No!' she exclaimed as Bill returned and bellowed, 'What you doing here this time of day, anyway?'

'They've extended my hours. We need the — '

'You're finished here, gal. You're coming home with me. Nobody's extending nothing for you no more.'

'So long,' Cass said. 'Nice meeting y'all.'

He left the saloon and strolled along to the marshal's office where Brady was sitting on his butt as usual in his swivel chair. 'Ah,' he gurgled. 'The wandering cowboy. Howja get on?'

'Fine,' Cass smiled. 'Caught 'em all, 'cept one the cavalry killed. Mission successful. Just waiting on the rewards from Jim Clarke.'

'Clarke? That big mouth? Ain't you got the prisoners with you?'

'Nope.' Cass unpinned his deputy's badge and tossed it at him. 'And, by the way, I've resigned.'

'What, you snivellin' useless piece of offal, you can't do that. Who you think you're talking to.'

'You.' Cass put his boot between

Brady's legs on the chair and tipped him crashing back. 'So long.'

* * *

The solid granite Wichita mountains reared up from the prairie country as he approached, standing like sentinels above the spring-fed lakes, streams and lush groves of trees below.

'It sure is beautiful country.' Cass sat the Palomino and breathed in the spectacle before riding on to Kiowa Lake. It had been a long ride and to reach the Coxes' cabin felt like a homecoming.

John Wesley had made a good recovery from his gunshot wound and he, Elisabeth and Audrey welcomed him after his long absence, but the girl-woman was shy and silent, nervous as a gazelle. She sat on a corner stool and listened. Maybe she was conscious of her last and best dress now looking more like a rag, stained by mucking out cows and goats.

'So where you planning on living?' John Wesley asked.

'Jim Clarke's offered me a job as deputy. I ain't short of cash at the moment so there's no hurry. In fact, I had a bit of luck on the way back here.' He nodded at the carpet bag on the floor. 'I used my line and hook to fish that out a rattlers nest. A dead man was clutching it to him real tight. Didn't seem to like parting with it. I guess I'll have to report it to Jim when I see him again but meanwhile I figure I'm due to a fifty-per-cent share. Take a gander.'

The Coxes goggled at the $500 in silver and gold coins. 'But where did it come from?' Elisabeth asked.

'Who knows?' Cass grinned at them. 'Dead men tell no tales.'

He slapped two gold cartwheels on the cabin table. 'These are for you. He won't miss 'em.' Then he found a parcel and gave it to Audrey. 'I got you a present.'

When she undid it and held up a pale buckskin dress, with fine bead and quill work on the front, her joy was evident to behold. 'Go try it on,' he urged. 'Some squaw must have chawed a helluva lot on that to make it so supple. That's why they lose their teeth early.'

'So,' John Wesley said. 'You want to take the girl? I should warn you she ain't exactly the brightest button in the box. She's hopeless at her sums and words, can barely write, 'Cat sat on the mat'. I've tried teaching her music so she can accompany my fiddle on her flute. But she makes a shocking din. No wonder the Indians never come near.'

'I don't mind,' Cass replied. 'General Nathan Forrest said he'd rather pick up a snake than a pen any day, and me, I'm like that, too.'

'What we're saying is that she's a little bit soft in the head,' Elisabeth put in. 'Must be her ancestry. A lot of them aristocrats are. The girl's hopeless at housekeeping. Every pie she makes sinks flat.'

'Why should I care what a gal's like in the kitchen,' Cass grinned. 'It's in the bedroom that counts.'

'Hmm, perhaps in a few years you might change your mind.'

'Don't think so.'

'Where will you live?'

'Might take over that old cabin along at Ketch Lake. Colonel Anderson's hideout. By the way, he had a good send off. More'n a thousand folks turned up at Wichita for his hanging. He didn't flinch, proud and arrogant to the end. 'God bless y'all'. he shouted 'fore he dropped. 'God bless the rebel cause.''

'That man,' Cox commented, 'aimed to be a martyr to you Southern Rebs.'

'I ain't a Reb. Wow! Don't she look a treat.'

Audrey had come back in the Indian dress and her moccasins and her pale cheeks coloured up as she twirled.

'Best thing is I still get to see her legs.'

Audrey smiled, delightedly. 'Are you gonna let us wed?'

'You know you ain't our true

daughter but we'll always think of you that way,' John Wesley told her. 'We give you both our blessing.'

'We'd better send for a preacher,' Elisabeth exclaimed.

'We don't need no preacher. Healing Woman says we can go up on to the Holy Mountain for a special ceremony and the Indians will make us man and wife.'

'What, that heathen tribe!' Elisabeth exclaimed.

'*You* don't need to climb up,' Audrey said. 'We could bring 'em all back for tea.'

'First I've heard of it,' Cass said, 'But it sounds good. You know I was talking to the Indian agent along there. He says they're planning to open all this western side of the Nations to one and all, but there's plans afoot to turn this area into a wild life refuge like up at the Yellowstone. If so, he reckons he might be able to put a word in for me to get a job as forest warden. We'd be protecting the beaver, bears, elk, maybe even the buffalo from hunting.'

'That would be lovely,' Audrey cried, clapping her hands. 'I could help you. I ain't int'rested in cooking and stuff. I'm an outdoors girl. We could live here happily for ever and ever.'

'With any luck!' Cass had to smile at her childlike voice. 'You're a sweetie. Let's take a stroll 'fore supper, shall we?'

They walked away from the cabin arms interlinked around each other's waists. He could feel the supple strength beneath his fingers of her spine and back. When they reached the stand of pines it was Audrey, this time, who pulled him beneath its shadowy canopy. He caught her, tightly pressing her up against the bole of a tree.

'I think they're glad,' she murmured, kissing his cheek, still shy of his lips. 'Are you?'

'I sure am,' he whispered. 'I'm real glad.'

AFTERWORD

In 1889, 50,000 would-be settlers raced at the starter's gun to claim their acres when the western section of the Indian Nations was declared open. It was the first of many subsequent such land runs. In spite of resistance to opening the eastern section by the five civilized tribes, finally in 1907 the whole of their land became united as Oklahoma — 'the land of the red man' — the forty-sixth state of the Union.

Today many pure-blood Indians still live there, proud of their ancient traditions, others have inter-married and their blood mingles in the veins of a good number of 'Okies'.

Today 59,000 acres of the Wichita mountains and lakes are preserved as a wildlife refuge where, as well as a prairie dog town and 200 species of birds and wildfowl, deer, elk, and one of the world's largest herds of buffalo still roam.

Other titles in the
Linford Western Library:

TRAIL TO THE CAZADORES

Mark Bannerman

The five men who set out into the desert, searching for Joe Hennessey's wayward daughter, are bound together by very different motives: from greed for the offered reward to compassion for the young woman. But after an Indian attack results in the loss of his companions — plus his horse and gun — Texas Ranger Duncan is alone. Astray in this vast, hostile terrain, he is wounded and afraid. To top it all, the Indians who took his compatriots may soon return to take his scalp . . .

NORTH TO MONTANA

Colin Bainbridge

When Buck Nation rides into Gunsight, he little knows what trouble awaits him. He has inherited the dilapidated Forty-Five ranch — but did its former owners really die in an accident? Questions mount, and Buck is bushwhacked. Is Selby Rackham, former cowhand at the Forty-Five and now the owner of the biggest spread around, somehow involved? With a woman, an old-timer and a scruffy dog as his allies, Buck is determined to smoke out the truth, whatever it takes . . .

SHADOW HORSE

Steve Hayes and Ben Bridges

The Portuguese slavers called him Sam. They tore him away from his homeland and put him to work picking cotton in the Tennessee Valley. However, the big, fleet-footed Zulu was nobody's slave, and to prove it, he escaped and headed west. Throwing in his lot with medicine show conman Doc Jonah, Sam started entering county foot-races to earn enough money to go back to Africa. But then his trail crossed that of Major Lawrence Devlin . . .

BADMAN SHERIFF

Simon Webb

When the citizens of Coopers Creek elect Ned Turner as their sheriff, they are blind to the deadly mistake being made. For Turner is a lawless rogue seeking to exploit the position for his own advantage. It will be left to mild-mannered baker Jack Crawley to set things right. But can he rescue his town from the worst badman sheriff Montana has ever known?

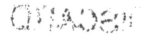

LONGHORN JUSTICE

Will DuRey

Cattle baron Nat Erdlatter has built his empire by taking what he wants, then ruthlessly holding on to it. Even now, with the Homestead Act encouraging people to claim their own portions of land, he believes that his needs take precedence over the government's decrees. But times are changing, and the citizens of nearby Enterprise are angered by his latest callous act — none more so than his ranch hands Clem Rawlings and Gus Farley, who become embroiled in an affair that can only lead to violence and danger . . .